Murder of a Late-Night TV Host

DEXTER JAMES

Murder of a Late-Night TV Host

Copyright © 2019   Dexter James

All rights reserved. No part of this book may be used or reproduced by any means, graphic, electronic, or mechanical, including photocopying, recording, taping or by any information storage retrieval system without the written permission of the author except in the case of brief quotations embodied in critical articles and reviews.

This is a work of fiction. All of the characters, names, incidents, organizations, and dialogue in this novel are either the products of the author's imagination or are used fictitiously.

OTHER BOOKS BY DEXTER JAMES:

Genesis Déjà vu – The Beginning

Genesis Déjà vu – The New Eden

Heist During the Rio Games

The Ultimate Conspiracy

Of Ghosts and Aliens

Ghost Marina on the Mississippi

Once More To

my wonderful wife Jean

Contents

Chapter 1 7

Chapter 2 12

Chapter 3 21

Chapter 4 30

Chapter 5 40

Chapter 6 69

Chapter 7 79

Chapter 8 101

Chapter 9 115

Chapter 10 126

Chapter 11 149

Chapter 12 154

Chapter 13 160

Chapter 14 166

Chapter 15 172

Chapter 16 176

Chapter 17 185

Chapter 18 193

Chapter 19 199

Chapter 20 202

Chapter 21 209

Chapter 22...221
Chapter 23...224
Chapter 24...227
Chapter 25...235
Chapter 26...240
Chapter 27...253
Chapter 28...257
Chapter 29...261
Conclusion...265

Wednesday 16th May 2018

Chapter 1

Favio Fearless, the notorious late-night TV host, was holding court in a bar close to the studio where he and his production crew had just completed recording his latest controversial, interview with yet another unsuspecting guest. The walls of the bar were covered in publicity photographs of celebrities, past and present, who had appeared on shows recorded in the same studio that Favio taped his shows. As was their want, once recording was completed, Favio, the producers and camera crew would retire to the nearby bar to discuss how well the recording of that night's interview had proceeded. At 11:00 PM one of the previously recorded episodes of their show would be aired on the network. The bar they frequented had numerous TV screens and the group would watch the program alongside the patrons of the establishment and the team would gauge their reactions to the interviews. Favio was sitting on his usual bar-stool at the corner of the bar, nursing a double scotch on the rocks. He was surrounded by the other members of his team, all of whom were isolating various snippets of the interview that had recently been recorded, vying for the ones they felt were the best. Favio was smiling at the remarks being made and it certainly sounded like another successful evening's work had been accomplished. Which was pleasing to hear, as his program had recently been syndicated which put much more pressure on him to maintain the standard. At precisely 11:00 PM, the chattering stopped, and all eyes turned to the various TV screens located around the walls of the bar. Favio was smiling in anticipation of positive reactions from the bar's patrons. Favio was a well-built man, physically fit, 6' 2" inches tall, sharply dressed in a made-to-measure suit, shirt and tie. He was a handsome man, dark blonde hair, blue eyes with sharp features that lent themselves to the small screen.

The familiar music, introducing the Favio Fearless show was played and Favio appeared on the screen to introduce that evening's guest. His guest on this particular show, that had been recorded a few days earlier, was George Fleming, whose claim to fame was the various books, YouTube films, and blogs he had created regarding a Vegan lifestyle and his opposition to animal cruelty during the manufacture of foodstuffs and cosmetics.

The interview proceeded along, following a familiar pattern, simple questions leading to a general understanding of the guest's background. Then Favio began to give plaudits to the man's tireless campaign on behalf of defenseless animals, a cause that he himself genuinely supported until suddenly, he began to backtrack and went for the throat. As usual, the barb came in a way that the unwary guest did not anticipate coming. During this particular segment, Favio produced a checkbook and said that he wanted the audience to participate in a collection to be made right there and then. He would match the sum of the audience's contributions and give it all to Mr. Fleming's animal charities, plus any donation that Mr. Fleming was also willing to make. Not wanting to miss out on such a lucrative opportunity, Mr. Fleming produced his wallet, which was his biggest mistake of the evening.

The wallet that Mr. Fleming produced was one made of leather and that was used as a springboard for Favio to highlight the man's hypocrisy. Obviously, Favio's investigative team had researched the man's background and knew not only of the wallet, but many of the man's other possessions. Artifacts, clothing, accessories, and shoes owned by Mr. Fleming that were made from animal products. Then, of course, there was his sports car with the seats, steering wheel cover, and gloves, all made from leather. The patrons in the bar were relishing Mr. Fleming's discomfort as Favio unleashed his typical verbal affront. Then he theatrically withdrew his checkbook and continued to admonish his guest.

At the end of the show, the patrons in the bar all cheered and applauded, some looked across at Favio's team and raised their glasses in salute. Favio and his team knew then that it had been another successful interview. Favio finished his drink, picked up his coat and briefcase, bade his team goodnight and went outside where he was met by a chauffeur who held open the rear door of a limousine to take him home. On arrival at his apartment building some twenty minutes later, Favio left the vehicle and walked over to the security door where he used his access key to enter the building before walking over to the private elevator that would take him up to his penthouse apartment. He waved briefly to the two security guards who were seated behind a desk in the foyer and they gave a polite wave back. It was 1:30 AM and the security guards weren't to know that they would be the last people to see Favio Fearless alive, except that is, for his killer or killers.

Thursday 17th May 2018

Chapter 2

The digital clock on the wall in the precinct was displaying 3:00 PM and for Detective Mario Simpson of the New York Police Department the day had been relatively slow and quitting time could not come soon enough. Simpson worked in the homicide division and he was looking forward to a couple of after-work beers at Clancy's, the local watering hole. In fact, he was just about to lock up his files and beckon his partner in crime, Pete, to leave, when suddenly, the familiar, dulcet, tones of his Chief were heard bellowing out his name from the adjoining office.

"Simpson get your arse in here!" Chief Horowitz called out, Mario knew immediately that this was not going to be pretty. Mario rose and hauled his six-foot frame into his Chief's office with about as much enthusiasm as a slave about to face a gladiator in the Coliseum.

"Yo, what's up chief?" Mario asked as he entered his Chief's office. Horowitz was a burly no-nonsense old-school cop, who in his day was lauded as one of the best detectives in the city. But now, after years of sitting behind a desk, he was overweight, balding and currently sporting a two-day stubble on his face. He should have been retired off years ago, but with a police district short on manpower and his reluctance to quit he was still there. Banter abounded that he had a roll-up bed under his desk because he always appeared to be in the office. The truth of the matter is, he is a widower with no children and the police department had become his life. But more importantly, he also happened to be very good at his job.

"Got a big one, a cold one in a penthouse suite down on 5th," the Chief replied and handed Mario a piece of paper containing a name and an address, "the victim's name is Favio Fearless and apparently he's a TV big-shot, a late-night TV host of some kind, so once the word gets out the press is going to be all over this."

"Great!" Was all that Mario could muster in reply as he reviewed the address and returned to his desk to retrieve his jacket. The jacket completed the ensemble of his tailor-made suit, a throwback to his father's advice, '*if you can't play the part at least look the part*'. The cut of the cloth accentuated his slim, well-built, physique. Mario was also a handsome man, dark complexion, dark eyes topped with an unruly mop of dark, curly, hair, courtesy of his Italian mother. But it belied a sharp mind and an inquisitive nature, courtesy of his English father, a retired fraud investigator at a major bank. These logical genes from his father had assisted him in becoming a lead detective at the young age of 33 years old under the tutelage of Chief Horowitz.

"We on the move boss?" Detective Pete Cannatelli asked, although the question was a moot point, he had heard the Chief's calls all too many times over the years and he knew something big was brewing.

Pete was Mario's sidekick, although over 10 years older than his boss, he complemented the tandem with an illogical abundance of useless information that seemed to appropriately feed solutions to situations. It could also be because Pete's mother is English, and his father was from Sicily, a perfect Yin to Mario's Yang. But that was where the similarity ended, where Mario was tall, slim and smart-looking, Peter was short, rotund and scruffy. Although in fairness, he had that type of build, complexion and longish, light brown hair that no matter what he wore, he would always look scruffy. In fact, he prided himself in the fact that he could look untidy wearing only swimming shorts. Today, Pete was dressed in a Beatles T-shirt, jeans and sneakers, a black hoodie, that was currently hanging on the back of his chair, completed his ensemble. Pete had risen from his desk and was just putting on his hoodie when a voice was heard coming from behind the two detectives.

"I'd like to come too, if I may!" It was a very tentative request, almost pleading, emanating from the desk in the corner of their open-plan office. Both men turned to look at Darlene Knight, a rooky that had recently been assigned to the department and more specifically, to their team. She had requested a transfer to homicide as a result of her fine police work during a drug bust that had gone down a few weeks previously. Mario and Pete had both privately discussed how the powers that be had connected the dots on that one, but nonetheless they accepted the addition to their team. "I haven't been to a real murder scene before," Darlene added.

"We don't know that this is a murder case yet, all we have is a body," Mario replied, "but sure, why not, come along. Just don't get in the way or tamper with anything, remember it may or may not be a murder scene. That's what we have to determine."

As Mario and Pete headed for the elevator, Darlene, in her excitement, was still at her desk gathering items and stuffing them into a large shoulder bag. By the time the doors of the elevator opened Darlene was still groping around retrieving items from her desk. The two men looked at each other and with a rolling of their eyes, they both entered the elevator. Mario pressed the button for the basement floor and the doors closed. It came as a big surprise to both men that when the doors opened onto the garage floor, Darlene nonchalantly stood there awaiting their arrival. She was smiling at them, giving no indication that running down six flights of stairs and arriving there just before they did would require that much effort at all. Sure, she was wearing running shoes, tight blue jeans and a NYPD jacket, that certainly didn't hamper her movements, but nonetheless, the two men were both impressed. Although they said nothing as they began to walk causally towards the unmarked police car assigned to Mario's team. Darlene's long blonde hair was tied up above her collar, as per regulations, which only accentuated her beautiful neck and features. In reality, Mario thought she was far too good-looking to be a cop and he knew for a fact, that was also what Pete thought.

Nothing was said as they all climbed into the car as if this kind of thing happened every day. Mario was driving, with Pete in the passenger seat and Darlene was riding shotgun in the back. Mario drove up the ramp from the carpool to the street and as they approached the exit, the sensor that controlled the traffic lights outside the police building sent a signal. Their light changed to green while halting all the other vehicles on the street. That meant that they didn't have to stop and wait for the busy rush hour traffic to clear as they headed towards 5th Avenue but it didn't prevent them from getting bogged down in the volume.

"Aren't you going to turn on the sirens boss?" Darlene asked, trying to contain her excitement as she was going to her first homicide, although she had to remind herself that she didn't know that it was definitely a murder case for sure.

"What for? The subject is dead!" Pete answered cynically.

"Yes, but surely the quicker we get to the scene the greater the chance of catching the perpetrator," Darlene explained.

"Again, we don't know that this is a murder case and even if it is, an extra 10 minutes is not going to make a spit of difference. So, just sit back and enjoy the ride." Pete replied casually.

"Yes, but at the academy –" Darlene began to counter but was cut short by Mario.

"Detective, Pete's right. Relax, there's a time and a place for hurrying to a crime scene, this isn't one of them. We get there all in a rush and all flustered you can't think straight. We take our time, arrive fresh and we can figure things out with much more clarity, anyway, the body is not going anywhere. This is the real-world Darlene, forget what they told you at the academy." Mario said.

Darlene managed to contain herself for the rest of the trip, which turned out only to be about 10 minutes in length, much as Mario had said it would be. On arrival, a patrol cop directed them to park their vehicle on an area of pavement that had been cordoned off with yellow police tape. Mario parked the car there and the three of them got out and viewed the scene.

"Hey Shorty, how's it hanging?" Pete said to the patrol cop walking towards them, Shorty stood a few inches shy of seven-foot tall.

"Keeping you in work Pete," Shorty replied, then pointed towards the building's entrance, "there's a private elevator just through the main doors and to the left. They're waiting for you in there." Pete waved a hand in acknowledgment as the three of them ambled towards the building.

Mario had a quick look up at the edifice and estimated the apartment building was about 40 storeys high as they individually walked through the glass-revolving door. The three detectives now had their IDs. hanging down on halyards from around their necks so that they were clearly visible. As a result, once they had entered into the foyer, they were greeted by a security guard cum doorman who directed them to a small elevator.

"There's only one button to press, it will take you directly to the penthouse suites on the 40th floor," the man said perfunctorily but politely. The three detectives entered the elevator and Pete pressed the button marked 'Penthouse'.

"Wow, so this is how the other half live, is it?" Darlene asked to no one in particular.

"The man said, 'suites' but the button suggests a single apartment," Pete said, pointing to the wording on the elevator panel.

"Probably just a slip of the tongue," Darlene replied.

"We don't like to hear a slip of the tongue," Pete said and made a mental note. During all this banter, Mario had said nothing, but merely studied the internal dimensions of the elevator completing a 360° search just before the elevator came to a stop and the door swished open.

They were greeted on the penthouse floor by another patrol cop that the men also knew, Tom Dzialo.

"Jeez, the gang's all here today," Pete said smiling at Tom. In response, Tom provided a theatrical bow, gave a fist pump to Pete then pointed them to an apartment door that was to the right of the foyer, about ten feet away from the elevator. Apart from the elevator and the door that Tom was pointing to, there were only two other doors on the floor, one of which was kitty-corner over to the left and appeared to be another apartment. The other door led to the emergency staircase that stood next to the elevator. Mario thought the foyer, with the absence of any windows, was of a strange design. Mario put that thought on the back-burner for now as the three detectives were led towards the apartment door on the right, Tom leaned over to open the door for them. There they could then see, lying on his back, the body of late-night TV host, Favio Fearless. On one side of him was an expensive satchel-styled, leather briefcase, the strap had remained slung across one shoulder where he had fallen. In his other arm, he had been carrying an expensive-looking raincoat. The victim had appeared to have just walked in through the door where he met his demise, the only indication of his death, that they could see was a small hole in his chest and a tiny amount of blood that created a red stain on his white shirt.

"Why is he lying on his back?" Pete asked rhetorically, "if he just walked through the door, why would he have turned to face where he had just come in from?"

"He must have turned or was forced around before falling onto his back after receiving the fatal wound," Darlene said out aloud.

Mario and Pete knew instantly that they had a murder case to solve.

Chapter 3

In addition to Tom, the policeman, there was another security guard cum doorman standing just beside the elevator. Tom explained to the detectives that his reason for being there was to assist in preventing any unauthorized personnel entering the floor, more specifically, he knew the people who lived on the floor.

"Hi, Detective Mario Simpson, NYPD, you are?" Mario asked the security guard.

"My name is Daryll Hutchinson, I am the security staff supervisor, I arrived here immediately after we received the call. I carried out a quick search of the apartment, just in case someone else was still on the premises, you understand. But finding the apartment empty I stationed myself here at the elevator until the other policemen arrived.

"Did you touch anything in the apartment Daryll?" Mario asked.

"No, I didn't even stop to look at the body, well, except to confirm it was indeed Mr. Fearless," Daryll replied.

Mario then turned his attention to the apartment, inside was another man who looked very agitated and continued to pace backwards and forwards across the room, the man was talking into a cell phone. Mario realized immediately that between Daryll and this other stranger, the crime scene had been compromised. Nevertheless, he insisted on the three detectives donning latex gloves and booties to at least minimize the addition of any new contaminants to the scene. Mario gave the apartment that was observable from the entrance a quick 360° glance. Apart from the unaccounted-for man he also noticed a slight aroma in the room, reminding him of the josh sticks, similar to the ones some of the students used to burn during his college days.

"Who are you?" Pete asked the man who was pacing inside the apartment.

"His name is David Johnstone, he discovered the body," Tom replied, "we told him he couldn't leave until you told him he could."

"Quite right!" Pete replied, "so, who are you?" Pete asked again as he gave the man a visual once-over. The man was short with long, blonde tousled hair, he wore jeans and a white turtleneck sweater and looked decidedly shaken. He immediately responded to Pete's question, ended his call and put away his cell phone.

"David Johnstone, I'm the show's producer —" David began, talking with a distinct English accent.

"What show?" Pete interrupted.

"The Favio Fearless Interviews," David said in a way that would indicate that you would have to have been living under a rock if you hadn't heard of the Favio Fearless program. Pete didn't live under a rock, but when it came to watching late-night TV shows, he may as well have done. With the responsibility of a wife and three teenagers, if he has the luxury of being home at a reasonable time, he would be in bed long before those late programs aired.

"So, what are you doing here?" Pete asked.

"I came to find Ivan," David replied, "Ivan is usually so punctual –"

"Ivan? Who's Ivan?" Pete asked, looking at David with a very confused expression.

"Favio. Sorry, his real name is Ivan Anderson, his stage name is Favio Fearless," David explained, "as I said, he's usually so punctual, he's a professional, so by 2:00, we were beginning to get very worried. We start gathering ideas for the show at two and rehearsals begin at three with the show being recorded at six. We like to be finished by 11:00 PM so that we can all retire to a local bar to watch one of the previously recorded shows that was being aired that night. None of our phone calls or emails were being returned so I drove over here to check on him and this is how I found him."

"Did you try texting him?" Pete asked.

"Ivan wouldn't have a cell phone," David replied, "he was always worried about the long-term effects of radiation, which can be absorbed by human tissue close to the phone. In fact, he was putting together a dossier with the intent of devoting a whole show to it. He just used a landline for phoning."

"Interesting. So, obviously you had a key to enter the apartment, right?" Pete asked.

"Sure, for just this sort of purpose," David replied.

"So, what did you do after you found him?" Pete asked.

"I immediately called the police, then building security and finally the studio," David explained.

"In that order? You sure it wasn't the studio, then the police?" Pete pressured him.

"No, definitely in that order," David replied emphatically.

"Has he ever been late before?" Pete asked.

"No, never. Neither here nor in the U.K." David said.

"In the U.K.?" Pete questioned.

"Yes, I worked with Ivan in England and when he received the opportunity to work over here, he brought me across the pond with him," David replied.

"So, he was a nice guy?" Pete asked.

"Depends on who you talk to. He couldn't stand that group of people who were born with silver spoons in their mouths. Ivan had to scratch a living from the day he was born, but if you were honest, working-class and worked hard, you would have no problem with him." David explained, "I never had a problem with him."

"When did you last see him?" Pete asked.

"After the airing of last night's show, around 1:00 AM. We were all at 'Studio 90', Ivan left, the rest of us all drank up and called it a night a short time later."

"Where and what exactly is 'Studio 90'?" Pete asked.

"It's a bar near the studio, go figure. It's on Corning and Main. After we had recorded a show, we usually go there to discuss what occurred during the interview. Then we start discussing the guest for the next day's show. Afterward, we wait for that night's show to appear on TV and we watch with the patrons to gauge the reaction of the people in the bar," David explained, "they represent a good litmus test for us."

"Did he have any enemies or someone who held a grudge against him?" Pete asked.

"How much time have you got?" David replied with a wry smile.

"I've got all the time in the world," Pete replied casually, holding out his arms to indicate lots.

"Just about any guest he's ever had on his shows," David replied.

"How many would that be?" Pete asked.

"Over the years, scores," David answered, "look, have you ever seen any of his interviews?"

"No, I haven't. Should I?" Pete asked.

"You would understand why the audience and TV viewers love him and his guests don't. He goes after the jugular and he is – was relentless. He embarrasses and cajoles his guests, he has a knack of knowing just how to push their buttons. It wasn't unusual for guests to suddenly walk off the set bellowing threats and talking of Favio one day receiving his comeuppance," David explained.

"So, who specifically?" Pete asked.

"As I said, it could be one of many," David replied, but then he looked briefly at his watch and began to plead with Pete, "look, I need to get back to the studio, we still have to prepare an obituary for to-night's slot. Is it possible for you to come to the studio at some point, I could provide you with videos and transcripts of all of his interviews?" Pete thought about that for a moment.

"Sure, is there a number we can reach you at?" Pete asked, and David handed him a card with all his co-ordinates. "O.K. we'll be in touch and you better warn everyone at the studio that we will be questioning them. Off you go then." David began to leave, but just as he reached the elevator, Pete called out to him.

"By the way, can you account for your whereabouts from the time you last saw Ivan until you discovered the body?" Pete asked.

"After we left the bar early this morning, I drove one of the cameramen to his home, he lives in Queens, then I went home to my apartment," David replied then added, "with my wife and young son. Drove to the studio at about 9:00 this morning."

"Good enough," Pete said and waved goodbye but couldn't help thinking that David's alibi was not exactly cast-iron.

While Pete was questioning David, Darlene had carried out a quick walk around the apartment, testing the door leading out to the balcony.

"I told you not to touch anything!" Mario shouted out from the doorway.

"Sorry boss," Darlene replied like a scolded child, "it's locked."

She also carried out a cursory check to see if there had been any indication of a robbery, all evidence appeared to be to the contrary.

As David the producer left the apartment, Darlene walked over to the body where Pete was now standing, eyeing the victim, particularly the wound.

"Man, you should see the gym this guy had set up in one of the bedrooms, whoa!" Darlene said, before turning to look at the body, "well, we have the 'who' the 'what' and the 'where'," she whispered almost imperceptibly, but it was loud enough for Pete to hear.

"Oh, you're going through the academy training thing again are you?" Pete asked sarcastically, "we don't have the 'who'. We have who was killed, but we still don't know who murdered him, do we?"

"No, we don't, but I think we can rule out suicide," Darlene stated, "there's no suicide note that I can find."

"That may not be a defining factor. Statistically, only one in six suicides are accompanied by a note," Pete replied, nonplussed, "but I agree with you, it's not suicide, the absence of any weapon would suggest that he didn't inflict that hole in his chest all by himself." Inwardly, Darlene was deflated, she thought she had added something meaningful to the investigation, but then admonished herself for not noting the obvious.

During all this time Mario had stood in the doorway, only moving to allow David to get past as he was leaving. Mario had surveyed the apartment, the entrance, elevator, emergency stairs and the balcony door across from where he had been standing. But Pete knew, he hadn't missed a word that had been spoken from the time they had arrived until now.

"O.K., listen up, we need to interview whoever is behind that door over there," Mario said, pointing to the only other apartment door in the entrance area. "I also want to check the possibility of someone entering through that balcony door, even though it is locked," Mario nodded his head to the balcony door, "I also need copies of the security footage from that camera up there, for the last 24 hours." Again, Mario pointed, this time it was at a surveillance camera located just above the elevator door. "We'll also need a copy of Fearless's phone usage for the last month. Pete, you need to follow up with David, you need to get down to the studio to review the transcripts of all the guests this man has ever interviewed. Maybe start with the most recent ones first and if any suspect jumps out at you, get their current whereabouts. Darlene, I also need to know the exact movements of this dead guy from the time he left the bar until his body was discovered and I want to know everything about him. Talk to everyone that was with him in the bar last night. Got it?" Mario asked. Darlene answered with a nod as she hastily wrote down notes.

"Once forensics and the medical examiner have done their investigations, we may have a better idea of what went down here," Mario added, "because right now, I don't have a clue."

Chapter 4

As if on cue, the doors of the elevator opened up and the forensics team led by Harry DeLuca entered the fray. They began to quickly don their protective overalls, not so much to protect themselves, but to avoid contaminating the murder scene, although it may have been a little too late for that. To give the forensic team free rein, the three detectives stepped out of the apartment temporarily and stood in the foyer.

"Hey there pretty boy, you've got lumbered with this one, have you?" Harry said, "how's it hanging?" Harry was short for Harriet, but it wasn't just her name that made her one of the guys. She was a no-nonsense investigator that just got on with the job. Standing at only five-foot-tall, she was a diminutive lady, but at 45 years old, with five children and being married to a cop, she'd seen it all, done it all and took no crap from anyone. She also just happened to get on very well with Mario and Pete, having worked on numerous cases with them. She was just cramming her vast mop of wiry, curly hair under her cap when she noticed Darlene for the first time.

"Hey, who's the newbie?" Harry asked cordially, to no one in particular.

"Hey Harry, how's it going?" Mario replied calmly, being used to Harry's idiosyncrasies, "this is Darlene, the newest member of our team."

"Oh, you poor thing," Harry said, pulling a sympathetic face, which unfortunately for Darlene was all that she could now see of Harry under her protective suit. She didn't attempt to shake hands with Darlene as she had just put on her gloves and Darlene was about to reply to her, but Harry's demeanor changed in a flash, "don't touch anything," and she walked right on by her.

"You got a warrant yet pretty boy?" Harry shouted to Mario over her shoulder as she walked into the apartment to look at the body.

"No, not yet," Mario replied.

"Well, it's a good job I did," Harry said, before adding sarcastically "you're welcome." She was closely followed by two of her team who were now also dressed in protective overalls. They were both men, but you couldn't have really been certain, except the detectives had seen them get dressed and because of the quick furtive glances, they kept taking at Darlene. A few minutes later the final member of the team arrived, the photographer. For fun, the photographer took a snapshot of the three detectives, but focused mainly on Darlene, the photographer also happened to be a man.

After a short period of investigating, analyzing and questioning, Harry decided there was not much more she could ascertain from the victim and she was prepared to hand the body over to the Medical Examiner, although, her team continued to carry out an in-depth search of the apartment.

As if he had been called from the wings, Humphrey Lazenby, the Chief Medical Examiner exited the elevator. Humph was bespectacled, short, and to be polite, a plump man with thin, wispy, hair. His 3-piece suit was rather crumpled, but as usual, he sported a distinct loud, colorful tie with the choice du jour being a jungle scene depicting a large gray-back gorilla in its center. The whole package made the man appear a little older than his 32 years, but, nevertheless, he was a handsome, good-humored and well-experienced man. Had to be to have achieved the position he had at his young age. He came from a rich Massachusetts family with roots tracing back to America's original settlers. They still maintained connections with family back in the old country. Despite his Harvard training, conscientiousness and passion for his work the first thing that he noticed was not the body of Favio Fearless but Darlene, he was always interested to meet a pretty lady.

"And who might you be my dear, apart from being a rose between these two thorns?" Humph said with a smile and a distinct Ivy League accent. He held out his hand for an introduction, "Humphrey Lazenby at your service."

"Detective Darlene Knight," Darlene replied and in turn held out her hand, taken back a little by the man's directness.

"Enchanted to meet you, my dear," Humph replied.

"Alright Humph, back to earth," Pete admonished him.

"Yeah, yeah. What have we got then?" Humph asked from the doorway of the apartment, "have you done here Harry?"

"Yeah, go for it Humph," Harry replied, "good luck, don't think there's much to go on though." Humph entered the apartment and got down on his knees to inspect the body. The three detectives also entered but kept a safe distance to let the examiner have his space. The detectives shared with Humph the information they had gleaned from David regarding the victim's movements prior to his demise, he took that in and went to work.

For a few minutes, Humph felt, prodded, poked and took a couple of samples before leaning back on his heels.

"It was raining this morning, I guess that's why he had his raincoat with him, but since noon the sun has been beating down on the apartment and the blinds hadn't been pulled down. Taking all that into consideration, my initial estimate is that the time of death was approximately 1:30 AM, it appears he was killed by an object penetrating his chest with some force, which I am sure comes as no great surprise to such intrepid detectives as yourselves. But what that something was, I won't be able to even speculate until after the autopsy." Humph stated, before continuing, "there doesn't appear to be an exit wound so we could probably rule out a gunshot, but the wound looks so clean and tidy. Some force to cause that neat a hole I must say."

"Will you be able to work on this tonight Humph?" Mario asked, "being a celebrity the chief is hoping to get some answers before the wolves are at the door."

"I'm not a celebrity, am I?" Humph asked, feigning surprise, then turned back to look at the victim's face. "Oh, you mean the victim! I thought he looked familiar. Isn't he that nasty interviewer on TV?" Humph asked, looking down again at the face of Favio Fearless. The others nodded.

"The infamous Favio Fearless," Pete said.

"Ah yes, the alliterative Favio Fearless from the eponymous Favio Fearless Show. Well, I must say, it looks like someone finally decided to follow through with a threat, hmph!" Humph said as he struggled to rise from his kneeling position, he took off his glasses and gazed briefly at the prostrate body, "you can have the body moved to the lab., come around at about nine-thirty, I should have some results by then."

"Thanks, Humph, appreciate it. Another scotch I owe you," Mario replied.

"Another scotch you say! It's up to a couple of bottles by now methinks!" Humph replied as he gathered his things together and began to leave the apartment, however, he couldn't resist a smile and a personal farewell to Darlene, "I hope you will be joining the detectives this evening at my office, my dear. Maybe you can join us at a local hostelry while these degenerate detectives settle their debts." Darlene blushed a little, but didn't respond, the others merely rolled their eyes, having witnessed many of Humph's previous romantic overtures.

"O.K., O.K., let's get moving here," Mario said, which prompted Humph's exit with a wave of his hand in farewell. "I'm going to interview over there," Mario continued, indicating the door across the way, then I'll come back to check the balcony and the rest of the apartment." Mario then turned to Daryll, "can you get me copies of the surveillance footage from this camera covering the last 24 hours?" He asked while pointing at the camera.

"Sure thing," Daryll replied, we use DVDs to store the data, we also have a reader you can use."

"Perfect!" Mario replied.

"But, there's just one thing," Daryll added looking a little concerned, "it's about Eleanor, Mrs. Emerson that is, who lives in the apartment over there," he nodded his head towards the other apartment door, "well, she is very frail. In fact, we are awaiting the arrival of Claire, that's her great-granddaughter. She is scheduled to move Mrs. Emerson to a palliative care center this evening. Very sad really."

"That's unfortunate, but this *is* a murder case and I **will** have to interview her," Mario replied authoritatively.

"I do understand that detective, but it may be more compassionate to have Claire in attendance is all I am saying," Daryll replied.

"You seem a little protective of er, Mrs. Emerson is that her name?" Pete asked.

"Maybe I am, I have worked here since 1990 before they divided the penthouse into two apartments. She is a sweet old lady, not a bad bone in her body." Daryll replied, but before anything else could be discussed the door of the elevator swished open, revealing a beautiful, young lady. The lady exited slowly, looking around at everyone in the area between the two apartments, visibly surprised by all the people in attendance.

"Daryll, what the devil is going on?" The lady asked as Pete pulled the door of Fearless's apartment closed, concealing the body from view.

"Hi Claire," Daryll replied, "it appears that Mr. Fearless has been murdered, I'm afraid. These people are the homicide detectives investigating the case." Involuntarily, Claire's hand went up to her mouth and her eyes widened in apparent total surprise.

"Oh my god!" Claire said, "when did this happen?"

"In the early hours of this morning," Daryll said soothingly, "look, I'm so sorry, but the detectives will need to interview your great-grandmother, a mere formality of course."

"I'm sure," Claire replied before turning to Mario, "I hate to be inconsiderate, but I have come here to take my great-grandmother to a home, is it possible to have the meeting as soon as possible?"

"Not a problem." Mario replied, "if you would like to go and explain the reason why I would like to talk to her, I will be along in a couple of minutes."

"Yes, of course, thank you," Claire answered, then proceeded to walk towards Mrs. Emerson's apartment to let herself in.

Pete and Mario watched, maybe ogled may be a better word, as Claire went to the apartment door. She was wearing a tight top and slacks that accentuated her hourglass figure. She fumbled nervously with the bunch of keys she extracted from her bag, then proceeded to drop them on the carpet. Obviously, still somewhat flustered by the news, she was then forced to bend over to retrieve them, unwittingly revealing the tightness of her thighs beneath her slacks. Once she had entered the apartment and the door closed behind her, the two detectives looked at each other with lascivious smiles.

"Voluptuous I think is the word," Mario said.

"Stacked more like," Pete replied.

"My God! Why don't you just come right out and say she's got big tits?" Darlene replied with some venom, not so much because of the men's chauvinistic comments, but more because, although very attractive herself, she was not exactly well-endowed in that particular area. Both Mario and Pete cried out a high-pitched 'ooh' and smiled. Daryll felt a little uncomfortable at the sexist banter about one of his friends being voiced by New York's finest, especially at the scene of a murder.

"I don't think that kind of talk is very becoming of detectives," Daryll said somberly. There was an uncomfortable silence for a couple of seconds, but the detectives didn't respond.

"O.K., back at it. Pete, take my car," Mario said, trying to take some of the tension out of the air, as he handed Pete his car keys, "you and Darlene go down to the studio, Pete, start going through the videos of his interviews." Mario instructed, "Darlene, you ask around and get the dirt on this guy. Go to that bar they hang out at if necessary and ask around, interview everyone who was there last night. Confirm what time he left and find out who brought him here, we may need to talk to that person."

"Or her," Darlene added.

"Well, that's what you have to find out isn't it?" Mario replied.

"Got it!" Darlene replied as the two detectives entered the elevator with Daryll.

"Oh, one other thing," Mario added as he held open the elevator door, "we need to establish if there is anyone who will benefit from

Fearless's death. Check with the producer guy, find out what you can."

"On it," Darlene said and made a note.

"Swing by here at about 9:15 to pick me up then we'll go over to see Humph, I'll stay here to see if forensics can come up with anything," Mario explained. Then he stepped back to allow the door of the elevator to close. Just before the doors came together Mario shouted out one more instruction, "oh and Darlene, touch base with Pete every so often, I want you to keep abreast of things!"

Chapter 5

A couple of minutes after the other two detectives departed with the security guard, Mario was knocking on the door of Mrs. Eleanor Emerson, the name given to him by Daryll. It only took a few seconds for Claire to open the door and with a pleasant but nervous smile, she stepped back to allow Mario to enter.

"Hi, come through, I explained to my great-grandmother what has happened, she is ready for you," Claire said, then she walked ahead of Mario to guide him to the room where Mrs. Emerson was waiting. Mario was taking in the numerous portraits and photographs on the walls of the apartment, there was hardly a spot that wasn't filled. He noticed that the layout of the apartment was not quite as open as Fearless's roomy place and subsequently did not have as much natural light. There was a musty smell about the place probably due to the old furniture, dust-filled vases and other artifacts that had been accrued by the old lady over the years.

"Great-gran, this is – sorry, I didn't get your name!" Claire said.

"Hi, Detective Mario Simpson NYPD ma'am," Mario said and even gave a slight bow as though he was visiting royalty.

"Hello, young man. What can I do for you?" Eleanor replied. She spoke slowly with a frail, weak voice, but her eyes suggested that she had retained all of her faculties. Her tiny, thin body was engulfed in blankets as she sat in a large wheelchair that housed a cylinder of oxygen with protruding clear, plastic tubes that lead up to her nostrils. Her appearance was gray and gaunt. Even without knowing what was wrong with her it was easy to see why she was being transferred to a palliative care home, she didn't look as though she had much longer in this world.

"I don't know whether your great-granddaughter has explained the details to you, Mrs. Emerson, but it appears that your neighbor, Favio Fearless, was murdered during the night and I was wondering if you were aware of any voices or noises occurring in the early hours of the morning?" Mario asked.

"I'm not surprised about what happened to him, he was a nasty man," Eleanor replied, "but no, I wasn't aware of any disturbances."

"Detective, as you can see from the door you came through, it is quite thick and the soundproofing on the walls is excellent," Claire said, "and because my great-grandmother's bedroom is at the back of the apartment; it is highly unlikely she would have heard anything at all."

"I see." Mario mused, "well, Mrs. Emerson, I don't think I have any further questions for you, I will take my leave and wish you well."

Mario rose and left the room, closely followed by Claire. Once they reached the apartment door Mario turned to Claire and in a more subdued voice so that Mrs. Emerson was unable to hear, he continued with more questions.

"I hate to ask you this Mrs.?" Mario asked as he looked at Claire.

"Pearson and it's Miss." Claire replied, "but you can call me Claire," she added with a smile that displayed a perfect set of white teeth complementing her beautiful oval-shaped face that was framed by long straw-blonde hair.

"Sorry Claire, as I have said, I hate to ask you this, but as you have access to this floor, where were you during the early hours of this morning?"

"I fully understand detective," Claire replied, "I was in my apartment in Boston, I work as an actuary for an insurance company there. I caught an afternoon flight here today."

"Can anyone vouch for you being in Boston at that time?" Mario gently persisted.

"No," Claire replied hesitantly, as though in thought, "I live alone, although I did call great-granny at about nine on my cell phone, you could check my phone records."

"I don't think that will be necessary, but I had to ask," Mario explained.

"I find it is better to call her on the phone. It's a landline and it is always beside her bed. I used to just Facetime her, but recently, she's generally tucked up in her bed by 8:00 in the evening, watching TV, and she often leaves her iPad in the living room," Claire explained then added with a quick laugh, "as well as sometimes leaving the TV on all night because she fell asleep."

"Hey, don't laugh, I think we can all be accused of that," Mario replied with a smile, "so, with her iPad she's even into modern technology, is she?"

"Oh yes, we brought her into the 21st century a few years ago. With me being in Boston, Michael in Frisco and my parents down south it was a good way of keeping in touch with her. More importantly, we could see what she looked like, health-wise. I could tell by her demeanor that she has deteriorated very quickly during the last few weeks."

"So, it has been both a blessing and a curse," Mario said.

"Yes, but at least for a few years she was able to retain her independence by ordering groceries and goods from the comfort of her home," Claire said.

"Makes sense. Oh, by the way, you mentioned someone named Michael, who would that be?" Mario inquired.

"That's my brother, he's flying in from San Francisco. We are expecting him to arrive sometime this afternoon," Claire replied.

"Does Michael live out there or is he just visiting the area," Mario asked.

"No, he lives out there," Claire replied somewhat subdued, "he decided to move out west about six weeks ago."

"Well, I think that explains everything, I think that will be all for now," Mario said, then began to open the door, "oh, by the way, do you have a number I can reach you at, just in case I have any more questions?"

"Sure," Claire said, and she reached over to a table near the door to search in her handbag for a calling card containing her co-ordinates. They exchanged cards and bade farewells.

"Oh, by the way, which home are they taking Mrs. Emerson to?" Mario asked.

"The Belvedere Palliative Care Hospice," Claire replied, "hopefully we can get her there this evening, at a reasonable time."

"Why won't you be able to get her there at a reasonable time?" Mario inquired.

"Transportation availability and traffic," Claire responded with some resignation.

"Call the home and arrange the transport and I will have a squad car run block for you," Mario replied casually.

"You can do that?" Claire asked with a surprised look on her face.

"Sure can, you are both important witnesses in a high-profile murder case," Mario offered and was delighted to see a warm, gratifying, smile appear on Claire's face.

After helping Claire out with her transportation issues, Mario returned to Fearless's apartment to find Daryll waiting for him with the DVD reader and screen. The apparatus looked like a small notebook computer, but its only function was to read and display the surveillance DVDs.

"Look Daryll, sorry abut the remarks earlier, but in our job sometimes joking around helps to alleviate some of the pressure, we didn't mean any disrespect by it O.K.?"   Mario explained to Daryll who accepted his apology with a nod, but he remained somewhat stoic.

"My partner downstairs has been reviewing the DVDs and it appears the only people who have entered this area prior to the time of the murder are Mr. Fearless himself and his cleaner, Anne, who entered the apartment at 10:15 and left at 11:50. She has a regular routine here, comes in every day at 10:15 to make sure Mr. Fearless is awake, then prepares breakfast for him and makes his bed. A couple of days a week she also carries out cleaning chores. She has other clients in the building, including Mrs. Emerson, but Mr. Fearless and Mrs. Emerson are the only ones she actually cooks for. After leaving Mr. Fearless's apartment she generally goes straight over to Mrs. Emerson's to prepare lunch for her. But I'm sure you will want to interview her and review the DVDs for yourself." Daryll said and handed Mario the equipment.

"Wait a minute, you say she came in every day to wake Fearless?" Mario asked.

"That's right!" Daryll replied, "according to Anne he's normally up and about by the time she arrives."

"So, why didn't she make an appearance in his apartment this morning?" Mario asked.

"Apparently, she had a doctor's appointment this morning," Daryll replied coolly, "one of her other clients asked me if I had heard how she was today, that's how I know."

"I see. Thanks, Daryll, good work, have you ever been in the force?" Mario asked.

"No," Daryll replied with an embarrassed laugh, "no, worked here and there until I landed this gig and I'm still here 28 years later."

"Well, thanks again, I'll probably have a few more questions for you later. But for now, can you tell me when the security guards who were on duty during the night will be back on duty?" Mario asked.

"That would have been Fred and Brad, they will be back on duty at 6:00 tonight. We have an eight-man shift rotation system that involves a week of nightly twelve-hour shifts, three days off, followed by six-hour day shifts and six-hour evening shifts. We have about a dozen security guards that rotate these shifts, plus me. We can also bring in some part-timers that we keep on the books just in case of an emergency, vacations, sickness that sort of thing," Daryll explained.

"Sounds like a complicated system," Mario responded with a furrowed brow trying to work out the shift pattern.

"It is, but the guys like it," Daryll replied, "it's structured so that it optimizes their free time yet still gets in their weekly hours."

"When was the last time you used the part-timers as opposed to the regulars?" Mario asked.

"Ooh, when would that be," Daryll said as he looked skyward and brought his finger to his mouth as he contemplated that question, "must have been a good three weeks ago I think, but I can confirm that for you."

"Thanks, but if it was that far back, it's probably not relevant. But, back to last night, so, you were not on duty last night?" Mario asked.

"No, that's right, as I mentioned, I'm the supervisor. Generally, I only work during the day, yesterday I left at about 5:30 and I was at home with my wife." Daryll replied.

"Of course." Mario said, "thanks again for this," holding up the DVD reader.

Daryll had to wait for the mortuary crew to exit the elevator, they had just arrived to take Fearless's body to Humph's laboratory. Good job it wasn't a little later, Mario thought, had Mrs. Emerson, in her current state of health, been leaving at the same time they may have got confused with which body to take. The crew was having difficulty extracting the stretcher out of the elevator. The gurney had to be upturned to fit into the small dimensions of the elevator. Daryll was providing some assistance as he couldn't leave the floor until they were out of there. The photographer was just completing his pictures of the scene, trying to get images from all angles when he finally gave the mortuary crew the go-ahead to remove the remains of Mr. Fearless, leaving behind just the chalk mark outline of where he was once lying after his demise.

Mario waited for the mortuary team to remove the body not wishing to look to see how they were going to manage to get the stretcher and the body into that small elevator but manage it they did.

Harry's team was still working the place, so he decided to have another check around the apartment before reviewing the DVD, making sure he kept out of the forensic team's way. Nothing had been ransacked, so confirming Darlene's thoughts, it appeared burglary had not been a motive. The balcony door was solid and locked from the inside, he would have thought it impossible for anyone to have entered without breaking glass or disturbing something. Furthermore, there was a little, undisturbed dust on the track, someone should have a word with Anne the cleaner about that. But more importantly, what it indicated was that the door hadn't been opened for some considerable time. Mario then went through all the rooms in the apartment, checking the kitchen, the living room with its spectacular views, the two bedrooms and the den. The first bedroom contained a king-size bed, it was adequately furnished, but nothing too elaborate, it also included a walk-in closet and bathroom suite. The same couldn't be said of the other bedroom, the one containing the gym that Darlene had commented on earlier.

Mario just stood in awe for a couple of minutes gazing at all the expensive equipment, it would have befitted one of the top spas in Manhattan. There was a shower area, the shower unit contained multiple shower heads with different settings available. The toilet area also housed a bidet and wash-basin, next to this unit was a state-of-the-art hot tub. One wall of the bedroom contained free weights and in the middle of the room was positioned the cardio equipment, treadmill, elliptical machine, standing bike, and stepping machine. There was also an expensive spin cycle that with Wi-Fi could be connected to various on-line classes. No wonder this guy looked so fit, Mario thought to himself, then decided he really did have to get back to the gym on a regular basis. Across the other wall were stored Kettlebell weights, medicine balls, Swiss balls, bands and other equipment Mario didn't even recognize.

Reluctantly, he left the gym to reconnoiter the rest of the apartment, he briefly checked out the den with its stereo equipment and big screen TV then he inspected the walls and ceilings for any possible entry points. Mario walked over to the front door and simulated a fall back into the marked silhouette where the body had once been. He lay there for a few seconds gazing around at the various angles of the apartment and the focal point, which was the front door, hoping for some inspiration.

"Taking a break there pretty boy?" Harry kidded him, knowing perfectly well what Mario was trying to achieve, Mario chose to ignore her, especially as the little exercise bought him nothing. With an effort, he struggled back to his feet and not for the first time that day reminded himself that he really did have to get back to the gym on a regular basis.

Mario sat down on a breakfast chair at the spacious kitchen counter and began to review the DVDs. After a couple of hours of fast-forwarding, rewinding and stopping at various tracks, especially at the time of the arrival of Mr. Fearless, which, according to the time being displayed on the screen, would have been about the time Humph estimated he was killed. Mario watched the other DVD he had been given, but after reviewing the times he figured that each one contained 12 hours of data. The two DVDs he was in possession of were both from midnight to noon, so he appeared to be missing the noon to midnight DVD immediately before the murder. He would discuss that with Daryll next time he saw him. He quickly scanned through that DVD anyway and confirmed Daryll's partner's findings, only Anne the cleaner had entered the apartment earlier the previous day, at least up until noon, which was when the DVD ran until. On that DVD there was also a clip of Fearless arriving home the previous day at approximately the same time in the morning as when he was murdered. Mario was a little despondent, he had nada, so he carried out another walk around the various rooms, checking cupboards, drawers, and cubbyholes before stepping out of the apartment. He paused in the entranceway for a while and carried out yet another 360° search that yielded no new answers. He walked over to both the fire exit and the elevator, but neither provided a line of sight to Fearless's apartment.

Next, Mario wanted to check how easily the apartment door closed by itself. First, he verified that he had in his possession the correct key to the apartment door, he went into the foyer and let the door close shut behind him. The big yellow police tape plastering the door was now clearly visible, but it was the ease of the closing of the door that impressed him. As he stood there staring at the closed door, he could hear the approach of the elevator climbing up the shaft. The door opened, and much to his pleasant surprise, Claire began to exit.

"That was a quick trip, wasn't it?" Mario asked.

"Sure was, thanks to you and the police escort, we arrived at the home in no time," Claire replied with a sincere smile, "I got her settled in, then, fortunately, my parents finally arrived. I needed to get back here to make up the beds for them, but I didn't want to leave my great-grandmother all alone."

"You said your parents live down south, whereabouts exactly?" Mario asked.

"Yes, they moved down to Florida once they retired, Punta Gorda to be exact, and they took the last two days to drive up here, so I wasn't sure what time to expect them." Claire replied, "look, I'm starving, you must be hungry too, can I fix you a sandwich and a coffee maybe?"

"Come to think of it, I am hungry, haven't eaten since lunchtime," Mario said, "thanks, that would hit the spot. Just give me a sec." Mario turned to unlock the door of Fearless's apartment and shouted out to Harry.

"Harry, just going to be in the apartment across the hall if you need me!" Mario shouted.

"What the hell would I need you for?" Was Harry's cynical response.

Claire and Mario then walked across the hall to Mrs. Emerson's apartment. Claire went straight to the kitchen to begin preparing sandwiches and coffee while Mario once more looked around the spacious but cluttered apartment. He scanned the many photographs that littered the walls of the rooms.

"I'm afraid the coffee will be instant; the percolated stuff is too fiddly for my great-granny," Claire shouted from the kitchen.

"That's the best, thanks," Mario replied as he continued to look around the apartment. It wasn't long before Claire came through to the main room bearing a tray containing two mugs of coffee, a plate of sandwiches and a bowl of potato chips.

"Sorry, best I could do at such short notice," Claire said humbly.

"Wow, can't imagine what it would be like if you'd had prior notice, this is excellent." Mario said, "in fact, it is magnificent." Mario picked up a sandwich, a small handful of chips and began to eat.

"I couldn't help notice," Mario said, after he had swallowed a couple of mouthfuls of his ham and cheese sandwich, "I'm a detective, remember, that's my job, there are some cigars in tubes over there. Surely Mrs. Emerson doesn't smoke those, does she?" Claire gave a quick look around to see the almost full rack of cigars that Mario was referring to.

"Oh, those?" Claire said between mouthfuls and let out a slight laugh, "no, of course not! My great-grandfather used to enjoy a smoke after dinner. After he died, great-granny didn't have the heart to throw them away, so they have sat there all this while. She used to say the smell of the cigars reminded her of his presence."

"When did he die?" Mario asked.

"November '93, it was a tough time for my great-granny in more ways than one." Claire recalled, "she used to dote on him, so his death hit her hard, but what was worse was that the business he had built up was in the midst of going bankrupt, so she was left with no money."

"What business was he in?" Mario asked.

"He was an insurance broker. He used to say that just after the second world war, as couples were getting married and having children, people were falling over each over to buy life insurance and that continued to hold true throughout the fifties and into the early sixties. But as companies prospered, they began to offer group insurance to all their employees and the demand for personal insurance declined. Although, he still lived off the commissions of all those policies that he had sold in the early years, but, as they became delinquent the income began to dry up."

"What did your great-granny do while he was at work?" Mario inquired as he picked up another sandwich and a handful of chips to place on his plate.

"She just pottered about doing her crafts, keeping herself busy and then in 1978 they moved into this place," Claire replied.

"It must have cost a good bit of coin to buy this place," Mario said, "I mean, location alone!"

"Not as much as you might think. Fortunately, in the early fifties, my great-grandfather had made some great investments in land, buying and selling upwards until eventually, he purchased the very land that this building is on. Some property developers approached him wanting to purchase the land to build an apartment block, so my great-grandfather negotiated a deal. In return for the sale of the land, he would receive a small cash settlement and they would build him a penthouse floor at the top of the building which he would own, outright in perpetuity. No rent, no utility or maintenance costs and if the building was ever sold the arrangement would be continued or his family would receive a portion of the purchase price." Claire explained.

"What a deal!" Mario said, genuinely impressed.

"But of course, after his death, it meant great-granny still had a place to live in but with little or no income. So, my father stepped in and negotiated another deal with the owners. Great-granny would sell half of the floor back to the owners in return for a monthly stipend, enough for her to live on comfortably for the rest of her life. So, they used the space to build a luxury penthouse suite and charge exorbitant rates that more than covered what they were paying out to great-granny," Claire explained.

"Ah, so that explains why it just says 'penthouse' in the elevator, not penthouses or apartment suites or something like that," Mario said with a kind of eureka moment.

"That's right, that all happened in '95. Since then we have had various neighbors, mostly good and Mr. Fearless moved in a couple of years ago." Claire said

"He's one of the not so good ones?" Mario asked.

"You could say that, nothing outrageous, just obnoxious," Claire responded, "fortunately, his schedule necessitated him being out at night and in during the day which was the opposite of great-granny's. Then, over time, she became house-bound, so they never really saw each other very much at all," but it appeared to Mario that a cloud had descended on Claire's face as she spoke about her great-grandmother's famous neighbor.

"So, when your great-grandmother passes, what happens to the apartment?" Mario asked with some curiosity.

"It goes to my parents, but now they have moved to Florida, they have no interest in spending the winters up here," Claire explained and then sat up straight, all proud, with a big smile on her face, "so, I will be changing jobs and moving in here and when my parents want to come to New York they will be able to stay with me. And before you ask, my brother Michael, who I mentioned to you before, well, he lives on the west coast and he has no interest in returning to this city and no, he hasn't left California for at least a month."

"Well, that just about gives me everything I need to know, thank you," Mario said as he finished his coffee and began to rise, "I need to get downstairs to interview the security guards who were on duty last night."

"Oh, Brad and Fred, lovely guys." Claire said, "just spoke to them before I came up."

"Just one thing, you haven't mentioned your grandparents at all!" Mario queried.

"My grandfather, Edgar Emerson, he left school and went directly into the family business to work for his father, consequently, because he chose not to go to college, he became eligible for the draft and unfortunately, he was killed in Vietnam during the second phase of the Tet offensive," Claire explained, "he never got to see his daughter, Angela, my mother. His wife, Avril, remarried and moved upstate leaving my mother to be looked after by my great-grandparents. Sure, granny used to come to the city a couple of times a year to visit and take my mother out for the day, but I think she was upset that she wouldn't be entitled to anything regarding the apartment so over the years we began to see less and less of her. We're not even sure if Avril is still alive or not, the family has now lost all contact with her."

"You say she wouldn't be entitled to anything, but surely as Edgar's widow, she would be eligible to inherit the apartment?" Mario asked.

"No, my great-grandfather had foreseen potential marital problems and made sure it would have to be a blood relative who inherited, much like the British monarchy." Claire explained, "and if the direct bloodline expires, then ownership of the apartment reverts back to the property owners. Although, the owner can still choose to pass ownership onto a non-relative. For example, if, heaven forbid, my mother was to pass away before my great-grandmother, then she could choose to pass ownership on to my father even though he is not a blood-relative."

"I see, I think," Mario said, "so your great-grandmother can't just give it away to anyone, like a friend or charity?"

"No, that's right, there has to be some close affinity with the person. Very much like having an insurable interest with someone when taking out an insurance policy. You can't just take out a life insurance policy on a complete stranger, there has to be consent and an insurable interest, for example, a business partner or an extended family member."

"I think I've got it," Mario replied, then he realized, time was moving along, "look, thanks again for the meal it was great, but I really have to go."

"My pleasure," Claire said as she rose to see her guest out of the apartment. As they reached the door there was a photograph Mario hadn't noticed before. It was a picture of a handsome looking man holding an oar while standing by a canoe.

"Who would that be?" Mario asked.

"Oh, that's my great-grandfather, Ralph Emerson." Claire said, "he was quite the character, loved the outdoors when he was a young man."

"You mean hunting?" Mario asked, "you know, game shooting that kind of thing."

"No, not at all, he didn't hunt, just enjoyed outdoor sports," Claire answered, "and as he got older, he tended to spend more and more of his time doing math puzzles, he loved numbers. Maybe that is why he was in the insurance business."

"So, did Mrs. Emerson ever participate in any of the outdoor sports?" Mario asked.

"Oh yes," Claire replied, laughing, "she would accompany him to the wilds of upstate New York or Pennsylvania. They would go camping, kayaking, fishing, even whitewater rafting back in the day. But she was more of a craftsperson. She could turn her hand to just about anything, stained glass, painting, quilting you name it. Come with me, I'll show you!" Claire led him through the main room into a workroom and there, hanging on pegboards on three of the room's walls were craft tools, tapes, wires of all kinds. These were supplemented by kilns and racks of colored-glass. Claire bent down and picked up an errant roll of colored ribbon that had rolled onto the floor close to the door, once more providing Mario with a glancing, sensuous view of Claire's rear-end as it wrestled with her tight clothing. As she rose, Mario quickly turned his attention back to the work-room.

"There must be a small fortune here in equipment alone," Mario said as he looked around at the tools, most of which he had no idea what they would be used for. In the middle of one of the walls was obviously the work-bench which supported a vice, a work board pock-marked with burns, solder and splintered holes from repeated drilling or whatever. "What would she need a soldering iron for?" Mario asked, intrigued.

"Many things, but stained-glass mainly. Wait, let me show you something!" Claire said and left the room, leaving Mario to gaze in awe at the collection of tools at her great-grandmother's disposal. Laser measuring rules, exacta knives, drills, files and scissors of all shapes and sizes. Claire returned with a decorative glass prism, it was about eight inches long and contained shells placed loosely in the sand. The glass on the three sides and ends were held together with soldered lead. "We once spent an afternoon on the beach at Coney Island and I collected some shells. Great-granny put the shells in a bag, picked up a handful of sand and when we arrived home, this is what she did with it all." Claire said with unadorned pleasure.

"That's beautiful, I've never seen anything quite like it," Mario replied. "So, did you inherit any of these artistic gifts."

"Absolutely not, I'm a figures person, like my great-grandfather. Maybe that's why I am an actuary for an insurance company. I can't draw a straight line to save my life and my handwriting is atrocious," Claire said laughing.

"Join the club." Mario said, "well, I really have to go, but I hope to see you again soon, I might have to make an excuse to come by."

"No, you don't need an excuse, just come by," Claire said with a demure smile.

When Mario left Claire, he had a little bounce in his step as he returned to Fearless's apartment. Harry and her forensic team had just about finished their investigations and were just gathering up their equipment.

"O.K. pretty boy," Harry said as she was removing all her clutter, "we're about done here. Not a lot to go on I can tell yer, but I should have some results for you in the morning."

"Thanks, Harry," Mario replied, "look forward to it."

"We are also taking away a laptop we found in the den, one of the tech. nerds may be able to hack into and discover some contacts or appointments that may help the case."

"Good thinking, thanks," Mario replied.

"Got any ideas on who did this?" Harry asked in passing as she was removing her overalls and gloves.

"Harry, right now, I've got nothing," Mario replied, shaking his head in frustration. "I was hoping that between you and Humph we could get some sort of evidence that would give us a lead."

"You never know, it's early days yet, chin up," Harry said and then she waited for her team to place all their equipment in the elevator, she gave a quick wave and they were gone.

Mario decided to have one more cursory look around the apartment. Satisfied that nothing had been left behind, except for the DVD reader. He thought that this would be a good opportunity to give Chief Horowitz an update, so he used the speed dial on his cell phone to call him.

"Chief Horowitz!" Came the curt response.

"Hi chief," Mario said.

"Whadda ya got?" Horowitz asked in that gruff voice of his.

"Just a dead body right now chief," Mario said, "got me beat at the moment, but we're working on it."

"Ah, early days yet son, but a piece of advice, if I were you, I would stay clear of the precinct tomorrow," Horowitz said, "word's out, the Commissioner has been on the blower giving me shit to get this case closed yesterday! It's going to be a media circus around here tomorrow. Stay clear and just keep me up to date O.K.?"

"Got it chief. I'll tell the others to meet me here at the apartment in the morning. We're meeting with Humph this evening, I'm hoping he will come up with something because to be honest, right now it's a conundrum," Mario said. Horowitz was sensing a feeling of despondency in his protégée's voice.

"Look, kid, you've only been on the case a few hours," Horowitz explained as gently as his gruff voice could be, "despite what the press might be saying, nobody expected an arrest today. Keep thrashing out the facts like you usually do, it'll come."

"Yeah, I know it will," Mario replied, "thanks chief."

"No problem," Horowitz said, before adding, "just bring in the perp. tomorrow!" They both gave out a brief laugh, said their goodbyes and Mario terminated the call. Mario then locked up the apartment, walked over to the elevator door, pushed the button and waited for the elevator's arrival.

Once Mario had traveled to the ground floor, he walked over to the front desk to introduce himself to the two security guards whom he assumed was Fred and Brad. He asked them a few questions and they began to explain what they knew about Fearless's appearance in the early hours of the morning, which was very little.

"We saw his flash limo pull up," Fred recalled, "the chauffeur opened the back door for him, Mr. Fearless got out, let himself into the building with his access key. Once he was in the building the limo drove off, Fearless waved over to us, but he didn't stop to chat, he never does, then he got into the elevator. That was the last we saw of him." Fred then looked at Brad for confirmation.

"Pretty much it," Brad confirmed nodding his head in agreement.

"Can you recall exactly what time that would have been?" Mario asked.

"It would have been about 1:25," Brad said, "the reason I know that is because I was just about to do my rounds, which is on the half-hour."

"And you saw nothing suspicious during your rounds?" Mario asked.

"No, and we had no reason to suspect anything." Brad said a little too defensively and a little too quickly for Mario's liking, "I don't know what else we could have done!" Fred nodded his head in agreement.

"Nobody is suggesting there was any wrongdoing on your part," Mario assured them, "just trying to get the details, but do you recall seeing anyone lurking around outside the building before or after the arrival of Mr. Fearless?" Brad and Fred looked at each other and they began shaking their heads.

"You said Mr. Fearless had to use his access key, are the doors locked after certain hours?" Mario asked.

"Yes, between 9:00 PM and 7:00 AM all entrances are locked; entry access can only be made by using a passkey or by someone letting a guest in. Of course, you can still exit without a key," Fred explained, "you just have to press the red button beside the door."

"What about access to the garage?" Mario quickly asked.

"The same system," Fred told him.

"Is that a barrier system or a door?" Mario inquired, "I mean, could a pedestrian bypass the barrier and just enter the building?"

"We have doors, and we have a sensor system that would alert us if anyone tried to walk into the building through an open garage door," Fred explained.

"What about other exits that may not be secured?" Mario asked.

"None, we take pride in our job detective, we are pleased to say we have never had a burglary reported here," Fred said.

"No, but you have had a murder!" Mario quipped and he let that fact sink in for a few seconds. The two security guards looked sheepishly at each other and then looked down at their hands as they fiddled with their pens before Mario continued. "Did either of you go outside for any reason? A coffee run, smoke break or anything?"

"No sir, neither of us are smokers, our food we bring in, and we have a coffee-maker on site. No reason to leave the building." Fred explained, "in fact unless it is for an emergency, break or for the purpose of carrying out our rounds we are not supposed to even leave our station here." He accentuated his statement by pointing down on the desk.

"So, neither of you went outside at any time during your shift?" Mario asked.

"No, we didn't," Brad said, beginning to look a little uncomfortable with Mario's line of questioning, as though he was a suspect. Mario could sense his uneasiness, so he decided to give them an out, in the way of an explanation.

"The reason I ask is that if you went outside it opens up the possibility of someone sneaking in without being seen by the surveillance cameras or without your knowledge," Mario said, "are there any outside perimeter cameras?"

Fred gave a little cough and began fiddling with his pen, Mario knew something was amiss.

"Er, yes we do as a matter of fact, but I don't think they will reveal much," Brad replied.

"Maybe I will be the judge of that," Mario said, "could you arrange to get the footage for me please?"

"Look," Brad began, "maybe I did go outside for some fresh air after one of my rounds, but I can assure you, nobody sneaked into the building while I was out." Brad was looking very sheepish as though instant dismissal was the next step.

"Look, guys," Mario began to say, "I'm not trying to get you into trouble with your company. I am investigating a murder case here, I don't care about what you two get up to or what rules you contravene. All I care about is solving this case and exploring all possibilities. Now, can you recall what time that would have been?"

"It would have been once I had finished the previous round, so about 12:45," Brad said. Satisfied, Mario returned to his train of thought with the surveillance system.

"So, let me get this straight," Mario began to ask, "after 9:00 PM a passkey is used, so presumably you have a security system that keeps a record of which key has been used and when?"

"Correct!" Fred said.

"But there is no record of anyone leaving the building," Mario said.

"That's correct," Brad said nervously as he began to shift a little uncomfortably in his seat.

"O.K., can you get me a printout of the access card usage from 9:00 PM last night up until the arrival of Mr. Fearless during the early hours of this morning?" Mario asked.

"Sure can, but that will have to be done by someone from the Admin. Office when they arrive in the morning. I'll put in a request, you will be able to collect it first thing." Fred said, beginning to write a note to himself.

"Thanks, that will be a great help," Mario replied, just then he saw Pete pulling up outside.

"Daryll lent me a reader to review the surveillance DVDs, do you mind if I hang onto it for a bit?" Mario asked, "it's upstairs in the apartment if you need it."

"No, you go ahead, we can use our computers if we need to review anything," Fred said.

"Great, catch you later, oh and don't forget to get me that outside surveillance footage and that printout," Mario said and left the two men wondering what repercussions were about to come down on them as a result of this investigation.

Chapter 6

So team, what have you got for me?" Mario asked as soon as he had climbed into the back of the car.

"Well, if you're looking for suspects, I've got a dozen of them," Pete said as he drove away from the apartment building, "I fast-tracked through the interviews our man Fearless had televised, man, David is right, any one of them could have done it. Our Mr. Fearless went for the jugular alright, no holds barred, he made some of the guys look so small and some of them are a big deal. The wolves in the audience were all baying for blood, they loved this guy."

"Do you think any of the interviewees are capable of murder?" Mario asked.

"Oh, yeah!" Pete replied, "he embarrassed them, big time."

"Yes, I understand they have a motive for wanting Fearless dead, but are they physically capable of doing the deed themselves?" Mario asked.

"Just about all of them," Pete replied, "so, what did you find out?"

Mario went on to reiterate the conversations he'd had in the apartment building, his findings during his search and the review of the DVDs.

"So, do you think those two security guards have anything to do with it?" Pete asked.

"Nah, although they were getting a little agitated during my questioning," Mario said.

"Must be as guilty as hell then," Pete replied, "who would get nervous with you questioning them?" Pete joked and then on a more serious note, "why do you think they were so antsy?"

"Not sure yet, but I asked for more surveillance footage from the outside cameras," Mario explained, "it was then that I found out that Brad had used a side-door to leave the building at around 12:45. Which apparently is a no-no, as far as his job description is concerned. And it is one helluva coincidence as far as timing of the murder is concerned."

"So, great, we have more DVDs to look through now!" Pete said.

"Maybe not, I think we can back off from those, for now, if we get desperate for ideas, we'll have to visit them," Mario said, "Darlene, what did you find out about Fearless's background?" Mario asked.

"I sat down with David and he gave me a history of the guy," Darlene began.

"I thought David had a show to prepare for," Mario inquired.

"So did David but by the time he had returned to the studio his team had worked on a compilation of the best of the Fearless interviews, which is going to air tonight, so that really didn't leave much for David to do," Darlene explained. "Apparently, Ivan Andropov – "

"Who?" Mario asked incredulously, wondering who the hell she was talking about. Darlene merely smiled.

"Ivan Andropov was Fearless's father, he was born in Whitechapel, London, July 1950, his father, Yuri, was a Russian Jew who had begun wheeling and dealing during the second world war. When the Russians met up with the Americans his black-market business blossomed, and he managed to finagle his way to Britain claiming asylum. His parents had been murdered by the Germans during the Pripyat Marshes massacre, he had been fighting on the front at the time, so didn't find out about their deaths until the latter stages of the war. He felt there was no longer any reason for him to return home to Russia."

"Whoa, how did he manage to claim asylum?" Mario asked.

"That was just a ruse, he had developed such skill at bargaining black-market goods with the allies he had no intention of returning to a communist regime where those skills would have been negated. He greased a few palms and voila, he was on a boat to England." Darlene explained before continuing, "he chose to live in Whitechapel, that's an area in London."

"I'm aware of it," Mario replied.

"You've heard of Whitechapel?" Darlene asked, surprised.

"Haven't you?" Pete asked, "it was the site of one of the worst string of murders by an unidentified serial killer in history. Didn't they teach you about 'Jack the Ripper' at the academy?"

"Of course, now that you mention it," Darlene replied, "anyway, about Whitechapel, as it was full of Eastern Europeans and Jews anyway, Yuri settled there but ironically married an Irish girl, Caitlin O'Shea, a Catholic of course. They had a son, the aforementioned Ivan, he, in turn, grew up and married an English girl, apparently married up a bit because she came from the suburbs somewhere. Anyway, Ivan decided to change their name to Anderson, thinking his son, Ivan Junior, aka Favio, would stand a better chance in life with an anglicized name. Meanwhile, the years were catching up with old Yuri, the grandfather, and now that it was easier to travel to what was then the Soviet Union, he decided to revisit some of the old haunts of his youth. Unfortunately, he chose to go in April 1986."

"What's the significance of that period?" Mario asked.

"The Chernobyl disaster," Pete responded.

"How do you know this shit?" Darlene asked with some frustration, she was trying to impress her boss with her fact-finding and Pete's intervention burst her bubble.

"I remember it, it was a big deal," Pete calmly responded, "still is."

"Anyway, Fearless's grandfather suffered badly from radiation poisoning and died, never returning to England." Darlene explained,

"Ivan senior died of lung cancer three years ago," continuing to read from her notes, "man, that's got to be sad, four generations of Andropovs killed off, all under tragic circumstances and now there is none left." There was a silence in the car for a few seconds until Mario brought them back to reality.

"Did you manage to find out if there was a will?" Mario asked.

"I asked David, it turns out he and Fearless shared the same agent and lawyer," Darlene replied, "he gave me the lawyer's number and I called him. David had called the lawyer earlier to tell him of Fearless's death and he told me that the lawyer and his team were going to be working round the clock, so David told me not to worry about the time difference. Well, I called the lawyer, he told me that there's no will, no descendants, no ancestors, he explained it was going to be a dog's breakfast to work out who the correct beneficiaries are. He was also certain that there would have been nobody who would have expected to gain from Fearless's death, as far as family was concerned."

"Good work Darlene," Mario said, which pleased Darlene, only to be deflated by Mario's next question. "But you still haven't told me anything specific about Fearless himself. What have you got on him?"

"Fearless, right," Darlene replied a little flustered, "well he joined the family business from a very young age, buying and selling goods with his father around Petticoat Lane. He too was always a talker, according to David, he even once managed to talk his way out of a prison sentence."

"What?" Mario said, "how did he manage to achieve that?"

"Well," Darlene began as she smiled at the thought of it, "David had heard this first-hand from one of Fearless's friends, who happened to be in court with him at the time, that he had been convicted of receiving stolen property. When the judge asked Fearless if he had anything to say, Fearless gave it to him. Apparently, he had told the judge that he was about to enlist in the army to fight for his country, the second Iraq war was about to begin and was front line and center in the news, but a conviction would be a blight on his record, and he would be refused enlistment. So, he pleaded with the judge to dismiss the charge to allow him to join the army, which the judge agreed to, providing he did so within three months. So, he joined the army and after his training, he was deployed in Iraq, where he fought, displaying great courage and served an honorable tour of duty, with distinction I might add. Anyway, while he was out in the Middle East fighting, he happened to be interviewed by a TV reporter. The interview was live and in the middle of the battlefield, the reporter asked him a question to which Fearless replied and I quote, 'what kind of a stupid fucking question is that? Is that the best you can do? How much money do they pay you to ask mundane questions like that while we are out here getting our arses shot off?

Who's your fucking boss? Here, give me the fucking mike.' I've got it word for word, David showed me the video clip on YouTube, it went viral. Anyway, Fearless proceeded to interview other members of his team as they were holed up in a foxhole, on behalf of the reporter. Apparently, the powers that be were very impressed with his poignant questions and interviewing technique. So much so that when he left the army, he walked straight into a reporter's job at the BBC and it wasn't long before they gave him his own TV show, then his career took off from there."

"Hey, that's much better Darlene, that's the sort of thing that's useful to the case," Mario praised her.

"Just one thing, I tried to find out where Petticoat Lane is, I searched on Google Maps but it took me to approximately the right place but there was no Petticoat Lane!" Darlene said, sounding a little confused.

"That's because there is no such place as Petticoat Lane, it just defines an area," Pete explained.

"So why do they call it Petticoat Lane?" Darlene asked.

"For two reasons, the sale of petticoats that was prevalent in the market," then he added with a laugh, "and also because of the old wives' tale that the barkers in the market would steal your petticoat at one end of the market and sell it back to you at the other."

"Jeez Pete, how do you know this shit?" Darlene shook her head in amazement.

"Because I'm a detective," Pete replied and both he and Mario smiled.

"You're making this up, aren't you?" Darlene said in frustration.

"No, really, I've been there. My mother is English, brought up in North London. When she lived there, she would often visit the market on a Sunday. She took me there once when we were over there visiting family." Pete said, "hell, we may have even bought something from Fearless's family stall, maybe even from him, who knows? You gotta remember, some of the vendors are notorious for having stolen goods on sale. A lot of the vendors don't sell the same type of thing twice. One week it may be saucepans, the next crockery, the next jeans. It's all about what's available that week, what had accidentally 'fallen off the back of a lorry' as they say over there."

"So, Fearless's court case regarding stolen property is credible?" Darlene asked Pete.

"You betcha!" Pete answered, "and Petticoat Lane is probably where he developed his interviewing skills, you haven't seen bartering until you've been down the lane."

"Well, that was another thing David said about Fearless, he could haggle with everyone, he had learnt to get by in about 10 different languages," Darlene iterated.

"Sounds about right, because the objective was to have an empty stall at the end of the day," Pete said, "maybe he didn't sell out one day, so that's probably how Fearless got caught in possession and based on what I watched during his interviews that's why he was able to have an answer for everything."

"Well, so far, we haven't got an answer for anything," Mario said, "using Darlene's academy analogy, we have the 'what', the 'where' and approximately the 'when'. What we don't know is 'who' did it, 'why' and 'how'.

Before the others could reply, Pete was driving in the car-park of the City Morgue, Pete parked the car and they walked into the dark, daunting-looking building to meet with Humphrey. As they walked into the lab. Humph had just completed the autopsy on Fearless's body. Under the bright operating lights, the body now lay cold, white and lifeless on the table. One of Humph's assistants was just washing away the last of the blood and viscera pieces that were scattered on the table. This wasn't the first time Darlene had been in a mortuary, she had visited one during her training while an autopsy was about to begin, she found the smell of the chemicals as oppressive then as they were now. But this was the first time she had physically seen the results of an autopsy with the organs being displayed around the body and the messy, bloody, remains being washed away. She tried to equate what was left of the body with what was once a person who the day before was living and breathing, entertaining people on television.

Mario and Pete appeared oblivious to the gory scene and the obnoxious smells.

"So, Humph, found anything?" Pete asked as the three of them reached the examiner. Humph began removing his bloodied apron, gloves and gown and walked over to the sink to wash-up. Darlene was determined not to show weakness in front of her peers, but she was struggling to keep down the bile in her stomach caused by the sight and the smell that lingered in the lab. as a result of the autopsy.

"I refuse to discuss this case with you until I have the promised whiskey in my grubby little paw," Humph replied defiantly.

"Alright, we'll meet with you next door, in your office," Mario told him, "I could do with a drink myself."

"I could do with a stiff one too," Darlene said, momentarily forgetting that she was in the company of three politically incorrect males and she immediately regretted her poor timing and choice of words.

Chapter 7

The office that Humph was referring to was, in fact, the bar adjacent to the morgue, a handy place to go to when someone is in need of reviving one's senses after the shock of seeing a loved one lying lifeless on a gurney. The quartet entered the bar and Darlene was impressed by the sheer volume of sport memorabilia that fair littered just about every piece of available space on the walls of the bar. Signed photographs of players of all sports as well as shirts, boots, shoes, bats and equipment that claimed to be from various famous players.

"Are all these things for real?" Darlene asked.

"Sure are," Pete replied, "Larry used to be an agent, knew all the players who donated stuff here. If he decided to auction this stuff he could make a fortune."

Larry, the owner of the bar was already pouring drinks for the others.

"What can I get you, ma'am?" Larry asked Darlene.

"Bloody Mary please," Darlene replied.

They received their drinks and after receiving a verbal list of the specials and what other delicacies were available, they ordered some food. They walked over to a vacant table in a corner of the restaurant. There was a small group of people way over the other side of the restaurant, but they were well out of earshot. Once the four of them were seated, Humph began to discuss his findings.

"The time of death I gave to you earlier is accurate, 1:30 AM, there is no indication that there was a struggle of any kind. The stomach contents of the victim contained a quantity of bar food and alcohol, consistent with what I understand to be his whereabouts immediately prior to his demise. But the biggest problem I have is with the wound, never seen anything quite like it." Humph paused as he took a swig of his drink. "The internal orifice that the weapon made is so smooth with absolutely zero residues, which is unique in itself."

"What could have made such an entry?" Darlene asked.

"Your guess is as good as mine. All I can tell you is that the best estimate of the diameter of whatever penetrated his chest would be approximately one centimeter. I can't find a grain of foreign bodies, which is most unusual, you would expect to see some fragments from the weapon used, even if it was only microscopic."

"What about DNA?" Pete asked.

"I've been conversing with Harry, as yet, neither she nor myself have identified any DNA other than that of the victim's, but it is early days yet," Humph replied, "we have taken samples and it could be a while before they are fully analyzed, but until then, that's the best I've got for you I'm afraid."

"You said earlier that it had to have been administered with some force, could it have been something like an ice-pick?" Pete asked.

"Yes, it could have been, but I still have a problem with that," Humph replied, "you see, the resulting orifice is as straight as a die, the result of an attack with an ice-pick would indicate a downward motion.

"Could he have been hit sideways? I mean, someone surprising him from behind the door?" Darlene asked.

"That's a very good thought young lady." Humph said, "and yes, that too is a possibility."

"Except, according to the surveillance DVDs it doesn't look like anyone entered the area, so how would they have got into the apartment?" Mario asked.

"Could they have already been in the apartment, holed up somewhere?" Darlene asked.

"I checked through the apartment, there was nowhere to hide, especially for a large man, which is what we would probably be looking at here, based on the height of Fearless and the force required to inflict the fatal wound," Mario suggested.

"But the murderer could have just waited in the apartment, then hid by the door and struck when Fearless entered the apartment," Darlene suggested.

"But so far, there is no evidence of anyone else being in the apartment, unless Harry can find something," Mario explained, "nor is there any evidence of anyone entering or leaving the apartment."

"If, as suggested by the DVDs that no one entered the area, is it possible that somehow, someone rode the elevator with Fearless and administered the blow in there?" Pete puts forward.

"So, what you're suggesting is that after being struck, he walked from the elevator to his apartment, then had the wherewithal to –" Humph began.

"Wherewithal you say!" Pete said with a surprised look on his face.

"Yes, wherewithal, to unlock the door, then after opening the door carry out a pirouette and fall neatly onto his back. All after receiving a fatal blow to the chest." Humph said, "the proverbial chicken running around after its head has been cut-off. Being a strong man, it is not beyond the realms of impossibility that Mr. Fearless carried out such moves in his death throes, but extremely improbable."

"Wherewithal?" Pete said again.

"Yes, wherewithal!" Humph repeated and took another sip of his whiskey.

"Looking at the DVDs, Fearless didn't appear to have been struggling to walk when he left the elevator, but good try Pete," Mario said.

"Well, there you have it," Humph said, "I would have expected a mortally wounded man would at least have been staggering."

"Could a projectile of some kind have been fired from the other apartment?" Darlene asked, "the other apartment's doorway is recessed so the surveillance camera wouldn't have been able to record anyone firing a weapon."

"Another good question, my dear," Humph congratulated Darlene and patted her on the hand, "possible, the trajectory would bear out the angle of the wound, but again, there is no evidence of any projectile, either in the wound or of one being left behind at the murder scene. Had a projectile of some kind been used it would necessitate the murderer retrieving said projectile and in turn, he or she would have been caught on camera."

"Unless someone was already in the apartment to remove the evidence," Darlene suggested.

"That would suggest there was more than one person involved in the crime. One to kill and one to clean-up." Humph replied.

"But again, how did the person access the apartment, then leave without being caught on camera?" Pete asked.

"Having met old lady Emerson I would doubt that she has the strength to lift a weapon, let alone use one and then be in a position to retrieve all evidence of it," Mario suggested, and he related all that he had gleaned from his meeting with Mrs. Emerson and Claire.

"Maybe it wasn't Mrs. Emerson, what about your girl-friend?" Pete asked, "she could have done it."

"Girl-friend?" Humph asked surprised looking directly at Mario, "what's all this?"

"Pete means Claire Pearson, she's the great-granddaughter of Mrs. Emerson and no, she's not my girl-friend," Mario explained to Humph.

"Yet!" Pete quipped.

"Anyway, she claims she was in Boston at the time of the murder, she called Mrs. Emerson at 9:00 yesterday evening on her cell phone," Mario told them.

"Does she have an alibi? It's a four-hour drive each way to New York from Boston at that time of night. If she paid cash for everything there would be no trace, she could have been anywhere, she has no proof of her whereabouts!" Darlene stated

"Well, tomorrow, when we receive the list of people who entered the building using their passkey we can check for her name," Mario suggested.

"What if she didn't use her pass key? What if she had been let in by your security guard when he went out for fresh air?" Darlene said, "timing could be about right if she pushed it from Boston. Depending on where she made the call, she could have already been on the road." Mario thought about that for a while.

"Again, possible, but unlikely," Mario replied, "besides, she would have been captured on the surveillance camera coming out of the elevator. All good suggestions, but nothing concrete and I hate to admit it, but it's got me beat!"

Just then, Larry arrived, deftly carrying four plates of food.

"Two specials, one Caesar salad for the lady and a Club for you," Larry said, laying the club sandwich in front of Pete.

"Never understood why it is called a 'club sandwich'," Darlene said.

"It stands for chicken, lettuce under bacon," Pete replied, as he tore open one of the accompanying sachets of mayonnaise.

"Get outta here!" Darlene replied, "you're making this up!"

"Maybe! I think it is a backronym because it is claimed that the first club sandwich was created in 1894 at an exclusive gambling house in Saratoga Springs, New York, called the Saratoga Club House. This theory is backed up by the fact that the alternate name for a club sandwich, as you may know, is a 'clubhouse sandwich'. However, other sources say Fraser Scrutton first made it at the exclusive Union Club of New York City. So, now you know!"

"Backronym?" Darlene asked.

"Yeah, one of those acronyms that was created to fit, after the fact," Pete explained. "You know, like the AMBER alert, you must have heard of that during your training, right?" To which Darlene nodded and mouthed 'duh', as she ate a forkful of salad. "Well, as you know it was named after the abduction of an unfortunate young girl named Amber Hagerman. Afterward, a national missing child procedure was introduced called the AMBER alert, 'America's Missing: Broadcast Emergency Response'. Ergo, a backronym."

"Jeez, how do you know all this crap?" Darlene asked, shaking her head.

"I'm from New York City, everyone from New York knows that," Pete replied, meanwhile, Mario and Humph just carried on eating as though these snippets of information from Pete were quite normal.

They continued to eat their meals, each of them mulling over all the facts that they had gleaned until Mario broke the silence.

"So where does this leave us?" Mario asked no one in particular, "right now, we have no evidence of a murder weapon and I think we have exhausted all of our options regarding how the murder was carried out. We are no closer to having any idea of what went down than when we first arrived at the apartment." The others didn't reply, their attention was drawn to an announcement being made on one of the overhead TV screens in the bar, the Favio Fearless show was about to begin.

Chapter 7

The familiar, signature, music, introducing the Favio Fearless show was being played, then a somber-looking man appeared on the screen to make an announcement. The man introduced himself as Francis Lewing and he was the CEO of the broadcasting company.

"Good evening ladies and gentlemen. As of now, I am sure you are all aware of the tragic news regarding the murder of our colleague and friend, Favio Fearless. I'm sure you are all as equally shocked and upset as we are, that is, the staff involved with the production of the show. We know the full resources of the New York Police force have been deployed and are diligently looking for the merciless killer of our good friend, Favio Fearless." At this last remark, the four dining occupants of the table all looked at each other surprised that they represented the entire NYPD. "We are confident that the assailant will soon be brought to justice," the host continued, "meanwhile, in memory of Mr. Fearless we have compiled a collage of some of his most popular interviews aired on the show, as judged by the number of letters, texts, and emails received by you, his adoring fans. Enjoy."

The screen faded to black and was immediately replaced by Favio Fearless beaming at the camera amid wild applause from the studio audience.

"Ladies and gentlemen, good evening and welcome to the show. Tonight, we have a sports theme, we have with us one of the great pitchers of baseball, New York Mets' own, Kyle McCluskey." Favio shouted out the last few words, stood and reached out his arm to welcome Kyle McCluskey onto the stage. The crowd gave the man a standing ovation with cheers and loud applause. Standing at six feet tall, McCluskey was a thick-set man, but had begun to get a little bit chubby around his mid-riff. He had a well-groomed college-cut hairstyle, the hair was dark blonde topping a tanned, craggily, face that was the result of years of being outside playing ball. He was dressed in slacks and a golf shirt. Despite beginning to go to seed, he still looked every bit a sports jock.

In the bar, one of the bar patrons shouted out, "great pitcher? The man's a bum and a troublemaker. That's why he's a journeyman."

"Good to have you here Kyle and great to meet you," Favio said as he shook hands with McCluskey.
"Good to be here," McCluskey replied.
"Well, now, you're playing those pesky Blue Jays tomorrow night in an inter-league game.

They're a good team, been to the playoffs or close to them the last couple of seasons, looks like you'll have your hands full." Favio asked, feigning a little concern on his face.

"By the way, this segment was taped during the Mets off day on the 14th and was one of those rare situations where they showed the program the same day. Apparently, there were difficulties getting McCluskey into the studio because of the Mets' schedule. It could only occur that night, so they decided to air the same day," Pete whispered to the others.

"I'm surprised they're showing it on TV again tonight, so soon!" Mario said.

"Apparently, it upset quite a few people, they received a lot of calls, that's why they decided to rerun it," Pete explained.

"They'll be no problem, I'm sure we will take them," Kyle replied confidently and the audience, made up of mainly New York residents, cheered wildly in support.

"But before joining the Mets, I understand you played on a couple of teams that made it to the World Series and you participated in numerous playoff games, that's impressive."

"Yeah, where he came on and blew leads," another patron shouted out, "he's a frigging waste of space."

"Yeah, I have been fortunate in my career," McCluskey replied, smiling broadly with great pride.

"So much so that you were voted to be the Mets' representative for the Major League Baseball Players Association. That's an achievement you should also be proud of," Favio said.

"Yes, I sure am, thank you," McCluskey replied.

"So, tell me, why is it that you were pushing for another strike prior to the players' agreement being struck a couple of years ago?" Favio asked.

"Well, as the representative for the club's players I was trying to negotiate better terms," McCluskey replied casually.

"Oh, I see. So, here you are making millions of dollars a year and you want to go on strike for more money, is that it?" Favio inquired.

"It's not quite as simple as that, Favio. One aspect of the problem is that rookies, contrary to what the majority of the public might think, do not earn nearly as much as the established major-league players," McCluskey replied.

"My understanding, based on information from the league's office, is that the minimum wage for a rookie is a half of a million dollars a year. That's not bad for someone who is under 25 years old, which most of them are," Favio stated.

"Yes, that's true, but let's face it, the career span of a baseball player is maybe only a few years," McCluskey explained.

"Well, let's take you, as an example, you are now 36 years old, been in the majors, for what? Let's say, fifteen years. What have you earned during that time, 25 million or more?" Favio asked.

"But it's not just about me is it?" McCluskey replied, "I represent all the players."

"Sure, but you just said the career span of a baseball player is short did you not? But you have earned enough for you and your family to live on quite happily for the rest of your life. And yet, you want more?" Favio was starting to get under McCluskey's skin, the audience sensed it and was beginning to bay for blood. Cat-calls could be heard and derogatory remarks were being made as the cacophony of sound began to get louder.

"True, but you have to understand, we are away from our families for long periods at a time," McCluskey replied.

"As are military personnel, truck drivers and emergency responders who also risk their lives every day while earning a lot less money than you do. And to add insult to injury, they then have to pay extortionate prices to go and watch you play to cover your salary," Favio stated.

"Well, how they spend their money is their choice," McCluskey quantified, "nothing to do with me."

"Wow!" Favio exclaimed and sat back in his chair, looking astonished at the cynical remark made by McCluskey. Favio knew that the gesture would draw a reaction from the audience. In turn, many of those in attendance began to boo and shout unkind comments at the baseball player, who continued to smile, but nonetheless, he was beginning to look just a little uneasy.

"I must say, I was not expecting such a cynical response from someone whose salary relies solely on the interest of the public," Favio said, shaking his head, "is that what the Montreal Expos thought during the strike of '94?" Favio asked.

"Not sure what you are inferring!" McCluskey replied.

"Well, just before that strike the Expos were the best team in baseball, heading for the World Series." Favio explained, "you were a rookie in those days, weren't you? And what happened? Because of the new agreement they were forced to sell all their top players, fans were disgusted, attendance fell, and they eventually had to move the franchise to Washington. That's why the majority of players feared another strike this time because they knew, the public had got fed up with all you highly-paid Prima Donnas constantly asking for more money! They were frightened it would set the game back years." The crowd was cheering now and McCluskey was getting agitated.

"That's simply not true!" McCluskey said categorically and loudly.

"Isn't it?" Favio replied quickly, "what do you care if fans no longer attend games? You're so close to retiring you can just disappear and count your money for the rest of your life, baseball or no baseball."

"That's ridiculous, of course I care. For the fans, the game, and the players. I love this game." McCluskey replied. "Hell, part of the agreement we negotiated was to increase pensions, especially for those players who aren't up there earning the multi-millions."

"Oh, I see, so you were negotiating for better pensions, knowing full well that any season could be your last. How convenient! Not only does major league baseball have the best pension in sports it probably has one of the best pensions anywhere. All a player need is 43 days of service and he is eligible, plus full comprehensive health benefits. Hands up anyone here who has a better pension than that!" Favio shouted out to the audience, which drew more jeers from them. "Look, I'm sorry but there's only one word for anybody who has those kinds of benefits and earns those types of salaries and still considers striking for more. That word is greed. Pure unadulterated greed." The jeers turned to cheers and loud applause.

"You don't know what you're talking about," McCluskey replied and began pointing his finger at Fearless. But Fearless was undaunted, he continued to turn the screw on the baseball player.

"On the contrary, I believe I have just demonstrated to you that I know precisely what I am talking about and I've shown you up for the greedy, money-grabbing, individual that you really are," Fearless said, "let's face it, you're only on the team to make up the numbers, when was the last time you pitched in a meaningful game?" That was a dart that really got under McCluskey's skin.

"I've had enough of this, you're not even an American, you don't have the right to diss me like this. You should be grateful that this country allows you to work here. Next time you listen to our national anthem just remember which country you are in," McCluskey said as he rose to his feet and began to glare at Favio. The security guards in the wing were preparing to come onto the set and intervene, if necessary, not that Favio appeared unduly concerned.

"Well, now! That would be extremely difficult considering your national anthem is sung to an old English drinking song. But that's something you are all too familiar with isn't it, Mr. McCluskey?" Favio said, looking up at the baseball man. McCluskey stood with his fists clenched in a threatening manner as he tried to intimidate his interviewer. After a stand-off of only a few seconds, McCluskey turned and stormed off the set amid cat-calls from the audience. The program went to commercials and that was the end of the segment.

"Is that true, our national anthem is an old English drinking song?" Darlene asked incredulously.

"Absolutely," Pete replied, "in the day, it used to be sung at gentlemen's clubs, it praised drinking and sex."

"How do you know all this shit?" Darlene asked.

"I'm a detective," Pete merely replied.

"A good drinking and sex song, that's why I'm always happy to stand up for the anthem, I say," Humph added, toasted and took another sip of his whiskey.

"On a more serious note," Mario said and then shouted out to Larry, "does our friend McCluskey really have a drinking problem?"

"Are you kidding?" Larry shouted back, "he's had a few benders in his time, the Mets are mommy cuddling him, they want him to retire."

"How did the Mets do against the Jays on Tuesday night?" Mario asked, returning the conversation to the table.

"Got beat 12 to 1," Pete replied.

"Did McCluskey pitch?" Mario asked.

"Nope!" Pete replied.

"So, he probably heard it from his teammates when they watched the interview and because he didn't get put into the game that had the makings of one very pissed off baseball player," Darlene said.

"Do you have any more skinny on McCluskey Larry?" Pete shouted out to the barman once more.

"He likes to drink over at 'The Pitcher', it's a bar not far from the Mets stadium. Apparently, he can get a little pickled some nights I'm told." Larry said, nonchalantly cleaning a couple of beer glasses as he spoke.

"The Pitcher, a clever play on words considering the bar was frequented by baseball players," Humph muttered.

"He seems to know a lot about this guy," Darlene said to Pete referring to Larry's knowledge of McCluskey.

"Larry is a walking encyclopedia when it comes to sports," Pete replied, "why do you think he runs a sports bar? He got tired of being an agent, working with young greedy kids who wanted everything before they had even met their teammates, so he decided to buy this bar. It was a dump when he first bought it, but he turned it into this, but he still likes to keep up to date with his cronies in the world of sports."

"So, getting back to McCluskey, he could have got so incensed that he went over to the apartment building and waited for Fearless to arrive home," Mario suggested.

"Notwithstanding the probability of instant death before Fearless reached his apartment, what about the weapon?" Humph asked.

"And how would McCluskey know where Fearless lived?" Pete asked.

"One thing at a time. What do you call those tools the baseball players have for cleaning out their cleats?" Mario asked.

"Duh, a cleat cleaner," Pete replied.

"And how big are those?" Mario asked, ignoring the sarcastic reply.

"Hey Larry," Pete shouted out once more, "do you have the bar team's baseball gear back there?"

"Sure do, why?" Larry replied.

"Would there be a cleat cleaner in the bag?" Pete asked

"I'll check," Larry said and a couple of minutes later he had walked over to their table with a cleat cleaner. Larry handed the object to Pete, who immediately passed it over to Humph.

"Mmm," Humph mused as he lifted up his spectacles to inspect the object. The cleaner had an overall length of approximately 9 inches with a 4-inch non-slip handle. The actual cleaner was made of steel, was quite sturdy and about one inch wide by 3/16″ thick. "Possible, a major league pitcher would certainly have the strength and technique to penetrate a man's chest with such an implement. The length of the object and handle would certainly support depth of penetration but if my memory serves correct, this shaft," Humph ran his finger down the instrument, "does not appear to be the correct shape or size to have inflicted the wound found in the victim. However, I am prepared to review my findings. May I borrow this Larry?"

"Knock yourself out, the team doesn't play again until Monday," Larry replied.

"I'll have it back to you tomorrow," Humph told Larry.

"So, the cleat cleaner is a possibility," Mario said, "Darlene make a note, we need to find out from that producer fellow, David, if he can recall telling McCluskey where they drank after the show, he could have followed Fearless. If he did tell him, find out where McCluskey lives, we may have to pay him a little visit."

By now the commercials had finished and the next segment was about to begin.

Chapter 8

A smiling Favio Fearless appeared on the screen and began to introduce his guest.

"My next guest is Soloman Friedman, a member of the New York Federation of Mohels and an activist in supporting Jews and their descendants killed during the second world war. Mr. Soloman Friedman."

The audience applauded as Mr. Friedman walked onto the stage and after a quick bow to the audience, he sat down, which was just as well because he towered over Favio. Mr. Friedman was a lanky, slim, six foot six inches tall, man with short dark hair and piercing dark eyes under a pair of rounded spectacles. He wore a dark blue suit and the jacket just appeared to hang on him.

"Shalom," Mr. Friedman said.

"Shalom," Favio replied, "now, I bet there are a number of people out there in the audience and in TV Land wondering what a 'Mohel' is! Well, let me tell you, it's a similar type of job to the ones most of us have, it's someone who has to deal with dicks all day." Favio waited for the expected ripple of laughter to die down, "you see, Mr. Friedman performs circumcisions." This brought another expected laugh out of the audience.

"That's correct," Mr. Friedman replied with a smile, joining in on the hilarity, "but that's only a small part of what I do."

"That's because it is only a small part!" Favio retorted, prompting more laughter from the audience. "All joking aside, I'm sure you're correct. But is it not true that even some Jewish people are beginning to show concern about the risks of circumcision and why in fact, it should even be carried out in this day and age? Aren't some couples even opting out of the procedure for their sons?"

"That is true," Mr. Friedman said with a slight tilt of his head, "but nevertheless, it is a tradition and the majority of Jewish parents still wish to maintain that tradition and ensure the Bris is performed. I can still make a good living out of it."

"Yeah, about a hundred grand a year, plus tips!" Pete cracked. Darlene just happened to be taking a sip of her beer at the time and almost choked as she began to laugh. Fortunately, a sympathetic Humph was there at the ready to pat the poor girl gently on the back.

"But that majority has begun to dwindle has it not? For example, I'm Jewish and it was never performed on me," Favio said, "after all, doesn't The Torah state, 'you shall not make any cuttings in your flesh on account of the dead or tattoo any marks upon you: I am the Lord.' Forward-thinking people argue that this passage contradicts the requirement for circumcision because it involves the cutting and marking of the genitals. This, they claim, is not consistent with Jewish law and values. What is your take on that Mr. Friedman?"

"Well, it's all interpretation and this is a point one could debate for hours," Mr. Friedman argued.

"Naturally, it would be in your interest for all good Jewish boys to be circumcised wouldn't it?" Favio goaded.

"If you are suggesting it's the money, I take exception to what you are saying," Mr. Friedman said indignantly, "and you would be mistaken. Sometimes I receive nothing at all for performing the Bris. Payment is not mandatory, it is purely at the discretion of the parents."

"Well, I stand erected, sorry, corrected, that's very noble of you, especially for someone who is in as high demand as yourself, because I understand you are a 'cut' above the rest." Favio continued to joke about the matter and received more laughter from the audience at the expense of Mr. Friedman. "But, let's turn our attention to a far more noble cause, your involvement with Jewish families impacted by the deaths of so many Jews during the second world war. Why, Mr. Friedman, are you so invested in bringing people's attention to the plight of these families?"

"Surely, it's self-explanatory, the murder of six million Jews during the Holocaust is something no one should ever forget," Mr. Friedman replied.

"Well, that's precisely why it is not self-explanatory Mr. Friedman. Which holocaust are you referring to?" Favio replied, feigning complete surprise.

"Are you serious? I just said, the murder of six million Jews during the war. The Germans were attempting to commit genocide, the complete annihilation of the Jewish race." Mr. Friedman replied, a little incensed by the callous approach that Favio was taking on such a delicate subject.

"Well, there have been many times in history where genocide has been attempted. Jewish people do not have a monopoly on that!" Favio replied.

"Yes, but this was the Holocaust!" Mr. Friedman replied vehemently. The audience, some of whom were also Jewish, had gone quiet, even the most ardent of Favio's followers would have thought that even this subject was taboo.

"Really? Let me explain why I am questioning your vernacular, Sir Winston Churchill published his version of the Great War in 1934, a few years before the start of World War II. In it, he referred to the Turks as war criminals and wrote of their massacring uncounted thousands of helpless Armenians — men, women, and children together; whole districts blotted out in one administrative holocaust. It is estimated that 1.5 million Armenians were slaughtered. So, you see, you don't have a copyright on the word, holocaust." Favio told his guest.

"But there were almost four times that number of Jews murdered by the Nazis," replied Mr. Friedman.

"Really? How can you be so sure?" Favio said, "it is estimated that six million people were murdered in the gas chambers. But were they all Jewish? Among them were non-Jewish spouses, gypsies, mentally and physically challenged people, Russian and Polish prisoners. They all fell foul of Himmler's hotels." Favio said.

"Don't you mean Hitler's hotels?" Mr. Friedman countered.

"Actually, no, there is not a scrap of written evidence that has ever been found, suggesting Hitler authorized any of the killings," Favio said. The tension in the audience was beginning to mount, this was a topic of conversation that they didn't expect to witness and were enthralled by it.

"How can you say such things? Hitler made anti-Semitic speeches, his book, 'Mein Kampf', it is littered with the so-called Jewish problem,"

Mr. Friedman retorted, "the mass murder had Hitler's signature all over it."

"But yet there is nothing in writing to support Hitler authorized any of the killings." Favio replied calmly, "nor did he attend the Wannsee meeting where the final solution to the Jewish question was discussed in detail."

"My God, you're an anti-Semite!" Mr. Friedman shouted, "you are one of those people who don't believe the Holocaust ever happened."

"Again, which holocaust? Let's assume for a moment you are referring to the millions of Jews murdered by the Nazis, well of course it happened. My great grandparents were victims of the Pripyat Marshes massacre in Russia in 1941. And as for being anti-Semitic, I must remind you, I am Jewish, well, at least half. What I am disputing is your claim of six million Jews being killed and the fact that you think you have the exclusive right to use the word holocaust!" Favio responded.

"I can't believe I'm hearing this," Mr. Friedman said, "how can you even doubt the figures?"

"Well, I deal in facts Mr. Friedman and it is not me specifically contesting the information, it appears that even the people who now run the museum, at Dachau doubts the figures. They used to display a plaque there that read 'Four million people suffered and died here at the hands of the Nazi murderers between the years 1940 and 1945.' Guess what? In 1991, that plaque was replaced with a new one that clearly stated only one and a half million victims, 'a majority of them Jews.' Even census documents do not support the number of deaths reported. Figures before the war and after do not support the high volume of Jews that were claimed to have been killed during the war." Favio said.

"This is ridiculous, even your reduced figures, which I protest, are totally incorrect, wouldn't that still be sufficient for the world never to forget?" Mr. Friedman asked vehemently.

"Oh, I agree wholeheartedly, we shouldn't ever forget," Favio agreed, "but nor should we ever forget the twenty million Russians who also died during the war, I'm of Russian ancestry. Why don't we do more to publicize those 20 million deaths, part of the estimated 50 million people who died all over the world? So, Mr. Friedman, even if your six million is correct, which I question, that only represents 12% of the total lives lost. That means 88% of the lives lost during the war were not Jewish. Shouldn't we also remember them?" The audience was beginning to see Favio's train of thought and began to warmly applaud.

"Certainly, but they were not herded like animals to their slaughter and then died agonizing deaths." Mr. Friedman replied passionately, his hands were on the armrests of his seat and he leaned forward, trying to use his imposing, large frame to intimidate Favio, but it had no effect.

"You mean like those countless Burmese and Chinese who were slaughtered, raped or worked to death by the Japanese. Or the Russians who died of starvation and hyperthermia in Leningrad. Should we forget those? Why is it that seventy-five years on, all we ever seem to hear about is the suffering of the Jewry during the war?" Favio said.

"You're a poor excuse for a Jew," Mr. Friedman said with a look of disgust on his face, "you're trying to sensationalize a macabre part of our history, all to obtain ratings when the truth is, you are really nothing but a racist."
"Not at all, this line of thinking stemmed from my boyhood, well before I ventured into the media. My grandmother was a catholic and whenever my grandfather started talking about the persecution of the Jews she would retaliate with the persecution of the Catholics and give him a hundred reasons why the Jews weren't the only faction of people who had been persecuted throughout history. But if you want to talk about being a racist, what about the Jewish Film Awards? What if I were to promote a White Anglo-Saxon Protestant film award program? They wouldn't allow it, would they? No, but it is O.K. for you to have your own little segregated series." Favio said, "so now who's a racist?" The audience was beginning to cheer now, the conversation was appealing to the more right-wing of the patrons.
"I am not a racist," Mr. Friedman replied succinctly.

"Is that so?" Favio answered. "Tell me, in your organization, how many gentiles do you have elected to the board?" Mr. Friedman said nothing and looked decidedly uncomfortable.

"Judging by your lack of response, I bet that means none." Favio said and then looked directly at the audience, "how many gentiles do you employ in your organization?"

"I'm proud to say we have numerous people with varying religious backgrounds working in our organization," Friedman replied haughtily.

"I'm sure you do Mr. Friedman," Favio replied, "amongst the service personnel." Favio paused for a few seconds to let that sink in with the audience. "The cleaners, janitors, window-cleaners and the like, but how many actually work in responsible, business positions Mr. Friedman?" Again Mr. Friedman said nothing, but instead of looking uncomfortable he was beginning to seethe with anger. After another pause with no response from Mr. Friedman, the audience was now beginning to cajole him and shout out catcalls.

"Again, I'm thinking very few, if any, Mr. Friedman. And you say I am a racist!" Favio said. A smirk was now on his face and the shouting from the audience had built up to a crescendo. Mr. Friedman stood up, and his impressive tall frame towered over an undaunted Favio as he remained seated in his studio chair.

"You should be careful what you say," Mr. Friedman said through clenched teeth, "I find your words insensitive and incentive, there are people out there who have killed over less." Then Mr. Friedman left the set amid cheering from the audience.

"My, my, Fearless certainly had no scruples, did he?" Humph said as he shook his head in disbelief, "now, I'm not Jewish, but to question one of the biggest atrocities in human history, well, that does go beyond the pale."

"And that Friedman is a big guy too," Darlene said, "could he have taken exception to the interview and decided to get his revenge."

"Well, funny you should say that," Humph began, "and what would be more apropos than to use an instrument used in a circumcision procedure?"

"You've got to be kidding me!" Pete said.

"On the contrary, I believe the handle on a Mogen circumcision clamp would match the approximate size of the wound." Humph then thought for a bit, "the only problem with that is, that it is loose, but if the perpetrator had some way of fixing it so that it would become a solid, straight tool, then it could have been used as a weapon I suppose. And of course, being a Mohel he is sure to have sanitation equipment that could be used to obliterate any blood or DNA from the instrument."

"Darlene, another person to add to your list and check out his whereabouts last night and the early hours of this morning!" Mario said.

"Right boss," Darlene replied.

"What I fail to understand is that if this man Fearless was such an aggressive interviewer, why would these people who are obviously held in high regard and position, even consider going on the show to expose themselves to such potential embarrassment?" Humph asked.

"My thoughts exactly," replied Pete, "so I asked David the producer guy that very same question. His reply was that all the guests are carefully selected and only those with huge egos are invited to appear on the show. Each one of them turns up believing they will be the one that will get the better of their host."

"Has anyone ever got the better of him?" Mario asked.

"Apparently not," Pete replied, "but there have been some canny guests that didn't allow themselves to be drawn in by the man's barbs, turned out they were the boring shows that never made it on the air."

The conversation then turned to more mundane subjects until the commercials had finished and the host announced the next segment that was about to be broadcast.

Chapter 9

Favio remained in a seated position as he introduced the evening's guest, "tonight's guest is a man who has served his country in Vietnam and continues to be an activist for the rights of G.I.s everywhere," Favio began, "but especially those from that controversial Far East campaign. So, let's give a warm welcome to Mr. David Grover."

As David Grover rode onto the set in his motorized wheelchair the audience all stood and gave the incoming guest a standing ovation. Favio adjusted the set furniture a little to accommodate the correct positioning of the wheelchair for the benefit of the cameras. Grover was wearing a military green bandanna to keep his long, straggly hair away from his thin, gaunt, face. He was wearing spectacles, with large, dark, lens concealing much of his upper face. He was wearing a military dungaree jacket emblazoned with various badges from Vietnam units and squadrons. His green military trousers completed his ensemble, with one empty trouser leg folded into his seated torso on the wheelchair.

"So, David, what's happening?" Favio asked cheerfully and with a friendly disposition.

"Not much Favio, earlier this week I discovered that my ID. had been stolen and various credit cards have been compromised," David replied, which was greeted with groans of genuine sympathy from the audience.

"Surely, he's not going to verbally attack this guy, is he?" Darlene asked as she finished up the last of her Caesar salad.

"Is he ever," Pete replied, laughing, "you just wait and see."

"So, if you have lost your ID. David, should we just call you Dav from now on?" Favio asked as he looked to the audience for a laugh. Some of them did chuckle at the joke, but the majority felt a certain amount of empathy for the guest and were a little uncomfortable with Favio's verbal attack, after all, he was a vet. and an advocate for veteran's rights.

"I don't find that funny!" David responded with a stern voice, trying to capitalize on the audience's sympathy.

"I agree," Favio replied, then his smile was gone, and he continued in a much more serious vein, "under normal circumstances, I wouldn't consider it to be humorous David, but like most of your life since you have returned from Vietnam, it has all been a bit of a scam, hasn't it?" The audience was sensing something, and they had suddenly gone very quiet, expecting that the boom was about to drop.

"I have no idea what you are talking about!" David replied, but he was beginning to squirm a little in his wheelchair.

"Oh, come now David, surely you do. You knew about a month ago that you were scheduled to appear on this show so to garner momentum for a plea of poverty you and a few buddies organized the credit card scam. You were hoping the public would reach out and send you cash. Isn't that right David?" Favio explained and waited for David's response

"That's simply not true!" David replied, "I have no idea where you are getting this information from."

"Really? Did you not mail fake eviction notices to yourself, have your buddies travel all over the state racking up charges on your credit cards which you then reported to the authorities claiming complete ignorance of the purchases?" Favio leaned forward as he made his claim. "I have the names here of some of your good, buddies. Would you like me to divulge their names on the air?"

"It's an ongoing investigation," David managed to reply quickly, "I think the authorities would rather you didn't mention them."

"Right, I'm sure!" Favio said, "in that case, maybe we won't mention the various 'gofundme' pages that have been set up in your name." Favio then leaned back in his chair and paused for a few seconds. Having now planted a seed of doubt with his audience he was ready to move onto the next incriminating piece of information about his guest.

"Fine, I understand, it's an ongoing investigation, so sure, let's move on and just talk about your work over the last 50 years or so since you returned from Vietnam. Your record, in fairness, is quite formidable and it must have been very rewarding for you to see some of the progress that has been made to celebrate the contribution made by a generation of soldiers during that war in the sixties,"

Favio said, now back to his most congenial self.

"It sure has," David replied, feeling a little more at ease.

"But I have a little problem with that also," Favio said, the brow of his forehead creased as though he was confused about something.

"Why is that?" David asked, sensing his interviewer's concern.

"I want to show a few video clips of you making speeches back in the day," Favio said and a screen in the theatre began showing vignettes of a younger David appearing at numerous rallies and demonstrations. "Now David, you notice at various times in these clips you point to your amputated leg emphasizing a point, usually when you mention the sacrifice you had made for your country during the war. Now again, isn't that a little bit of false advertising?"

"Advertising? What are you talking about?" David asked incredulously.

"Well, the reason your leg was amputated had nothing to do with a war injury did it?" Favio said, as the members of the audience sensed another attack and were on the edges of their seats, "it was the result of a motorcycle accident a few years after your return from Vietnam. What's worse, you were completely drunk when it occurred." The audience all leaned back as one and let out an audible 'ooh'. "But you continue to infer to anyone that wants to listen that your missing limb was due to a war injury."

"No, you're right, it didn't occur during the war and I have never said that it did," David said in his defense, "but it was still as a result of the war. The government didn't recognize Post-traumatic Stress Disorder in those days, I was a victim, I should have received help and if you had delved deep enough into my history, you would know that's one of the aspects of the war that I have been campaigning for!"

"And I have, and I agree, that's a noble cause, but the only help you really needed was not from the government, but from Alcoholic Anonymous," Favio responded vehemently, which drew gasps from the audience who had been beginning to side a little with David and were surprised at Favio's latest attack. "Your position in the army was that of a storeman, you were positioned miles away from the front line. You never saw any action during your entire tour, did you? You just got tanked up in the PX every night."

"But it was the war that did that to me!" David replied, equally as vehemently.

"Is that right?" Favio replied, "well, I've spoken to many people from your home-town, each one of them told me the same thing. Your pattern of behavior was much the same before you left to go to Vietnam. Getting drunk in bars, fistfights, in fact, I was told you were considering hightailing it to Canada once you were drafted, but your father got wind of your plan and dragged you kicking and screaming to the recruitment office."

"That's not true, my father was a World War II veteran, he was proud that I was about to serve my country, that's why he came with me to the office. I was proud too," David replied, sitting up erectly.

"Well, that's not what I heard," Favio said idly, "it was because of your father's impressive war record that you were given a cushy posting as a storeman and not as an infantryman on the front line. I was told that you were attempting all kinds of stunts to get out of enlistment."

"Rubbish! Like what?" David replied, waving his hand forward as if to dispel the stories.

"Apparently, you actually told them you had a drinking problem, but your father told them that they would cure that for you. You also tried mental instability, but that was not borne out by your medical records and anyway, they had heard all the excuses before because you really didn't want to be in the army, did you? Especially serving in Vietnam." Favio said.

"None of this is true," David said shaking his head in denial, "I was proud to serve my country. How would you know anyway? Sitting there in your comfortable chair what do you know about combat and the pressures of war?"

"Well, funny you should ask. I served in Iraq alongside your compatriots," Favio replied casually, "we saw action, real action and like me, they had volunteered to serve their country. Had you?"

"No, but I did serve my country, proudly," David replied.

"So you keep telling us, David. But for how long did you serve your country?" Favio paused for effect, "I'll tell you, two years and done. So you couldn't have been that proud otherwise you would have signed on for more. But you didn't do that, did you, David? No, you got the hell out of there as soon as you could and if they had have told you before you were enlisted that you didn't have to go, 'oh we have our quota you can be exempt'. Would you still have gone? No, of course, you wouldn't have done. Meanwhile, you let people think that you lost a limb while fighting for your country when nothing could have been further from the truth. What sickens me is that you have made a living out of faking being a disabled, war-stricken, veteran when there are true vets. out there trying to make an honest living and who really could do with the help."

"You have twisted everything, and I am sure you have upset a lot of veterans across the

country. If I was you, I would make sure your door is locked at night!" David replied and with that he wheeled himself off the set and straight out of the studio.

"Wow! He sure tore into him," Darlene said, "I've seen that guy on other talk shows talking about the plight of Vietnam Veterans, man, never gave it a thought that he was a con-artist."

"In fairness, like hundreds of thousands of others at that time, he still served his country, regardless of what Fearless had said, but yes, he did con the public, no question," Humph added.

"When was this segment aired, Pete?" Mario asked.

"Two nights ago," Pete replied, "that would have been the 15th, so, Grover or one of his buddies is a possibility," Mario said out loud, "and they would have had military training. Another one for your list Darlene."

"In light of the topics of the interview it behooves you to investigate this fellow, but honestly, he doesn't appear to me to be a possible suspect," Humph said.

"Behooves us?" Pete asked.

"Yes, behooves you!" Humph replied, "but do you sincerely believe he has the stature to commit this crime? I don't think he has the height, nor the strength required to deliver the fatal blow."

"What about his mates, the ones carrying out the credit card scam?" Darlene asked.

"Small-time, petty crime," Pete replied, "certainly don't sound to me as though they fit the profile for a murder that has been carried out with such clandestine precision. They would never have had enough time to plan a murder that left no evidence at the scene."

"You're right," Mario added, "time would have been needed to case out the apartment building, Fearless's movements and how the murder would be carried out. Darlene, keep that on your list, but put that investigation on the back-burner for now."

"Got it, boss," Darlene replied, making another note, just before the commercials finished and the host announced the next segment that was about to be broadcast.

Chapter 10

The smiling face of Favio Fearless once more appeared on the screen, he was seated as he began his introduction, "tonight's guest is a man who has served his country in the military for the last 50 years. He has had many tours of duty in active trouble spots all over the world and has just retired from his position as Chief of Security at the Pentagon. Ladies and gentlemen, a warm welcome for General Dexter Haverly," Favio said as he stood and beckoned in his guest. The audience was applauding as General Haverly entered the set. Favio stood to shake hands with the incoming guest and gave him a few welcoming words. The General's hair was in a short-cropped style, he was broad and tall, he stood at the same height as his host. The General was smartly dressed in a jacket, shirt, slacks, and a military tie.

"Good evening," the General said to Favio and then gave an exaggerated nod to acknowledge the warm applause from the audience, "thank you."

"Wow, what a great reception, thank you for joining us this evening," Favio said.

"Pleasure to be here," Haverly replied, "especially with a vet. Who, like myself, has seen action."

"Well, I thank you for that General. Now, where do we start, you have had such a long, distinguished career and you have obviously traveled all over the world participating in numerous conflicts? Which one of your tours of duty would stand out for you as the most memorable in your opinion?" Favio asked.

"Memorable in what way?" Haverly asked, "for example, my tour of duty in Vietnam was memorable, but not for reasons I would like to discuss."

"No, of course not, I guess, the most satisfying assignments, then," Favio replied, "in that, you achieved the objectives that you were sent out to do."

"In that respect, I think I would have to say the Afghanistan conflict," Haverly replied succinctly.

"Interesting, why do you say that?" Favio asked.

"It was justifiable after the attacks on the World Trade Centre and we went there to show the world that the U.S. was not going to sit back after almost 3,000 Americans were killed," Haverly said proudly which prompted loud applause and cheers from the audience.

"Yes, but wait a minute, almost 16% of those that tragically died were not Americans, they were foreign nationals, some of them were even Muslims," Favio replied.

"Oh, I think you're just splitting hairs here, it was still an attack on our beautiful country, and it needed an immediate military response," Haverly said.

"Well, I won't contest that point, but the fact remains, the victims in the towers were not all Americans," Favio reiterated.

"Well, that's beside the point. You asked me my most memorable assignment and that's it. I guess it's because we went there and kicked-ass, the Russians couldn't do it, and neither could you Brits over 180 years previously," Haverly explained in an attempt to curry favor with the audience. It appeared to have worked, as for once, they began to laugh and cheer at Favio's expense, but he continued, undaunted.

"But you did have the benefit of our experiences and we were there by your side, along with military personnel from about 12 other countries," Favio countered.

"Regardless, we would have kicked-ass whether you were there or not," Haverly replied, getting even more confident as the cheers rang out from the audience.

"I think our Mr. Fearless is getting his own ass kicked by this guy," Mario said.

"I watched this one in full this afternoon, as usual, Fearless is just positioning himself, you'll see," Pete said with a smile.

"Well, of course, you would. But the fact is, the U.S. is still out there, and you don't appear to have completely rid Afghanistan of the terrorists. There are still cells of belligerents fighting back," Favio pointed out.

"Yes, but we will eradicate them all eventually," Haverly said.

"What do you mean by eventually? It's been 17 years since you first invaded," Favio asked, "it looks like becoming the longest continuous conflict the U.S. has ever been involved in."

"Well, now that I am retired, I'm not in a position to give an opinion on that. All I can tell you is that we have been more successful than both the British and the Russians after they invaded Afghanistan," Haverly said smugly.

"Wait a minute, point of order, my understanding is that the Russians didn't invade, they were asked to go into Afghanistan to assist the government against rebels!" Favio said.

"Ha! You believe that Russian propaganda?" Haverly snorted

"Yes, just as much as I did when the Americans said they were asked to go into Grenada," Favio replied.

"Well, the U.S. was asked to go to Grenada's assistance to restore law and order and reinstitute legitimate elections. I know, I was part of that force," Haverly said, pointing to himself.

"Well, good for you General! So deep down you know it was exactly the same type of situation that the Russians were asked to go to war for, that is, to the Afghan's assistance," Favio pushed the point once more.

"No, it is not. In Grenada, the communists were attempting to expand their empire, that's why we were there, to prevent that happening," Haverly said.

"I thought you just said it was to restore law and order!" Favio said, "is that what the American public was supposed to believe? Or was the invasion because President Reagan believed that the presence of Cubans and the building of a new airport on the island supported the Soviets?"

"We were asked to go to Grenada's assistance!" Was all that Haverly would reply.

"So, the fact that there was a large Cuban presence on the island had nothing to do with the decision then?" Favio asked.

"What if it did? It doesn't matter, we were asked, the Russians weren't," Haverly said.

"How do you know the Russians weren't asked?" Favio goaded the General.

"The Russians were too busy elsewhere, aggressively attempting to expand their empire and promote communism, they wanted to occupy every country in the world," Haverly said with a grimace as though he detested the Russians with a passion.

"Really?" Favio simply said, "since the Afghan war, the old Soviet Union has dissolved. How many countries do you think are occupied by Russian troops in today's world General?"

Haverly thought for a moment, then replied, "I have no idea!"

"I can tell you, nine countries, give or take. However, all but three of those nations are countries that were part of the old Soviet Union," Favio paused to let that information sink in, "now, how many countries do you think there are where the U.S. has a military presence?"

This time, Haverly didn't pause, "I wouldn't know."

"Well, you might be surprised to know that the U.S. has troops in 150 countries," Favio said, accentuating the count and producing gasps from the audience.

"Some 165,000 personnel are based in these 150 countries," Favio explained, "so, do you still say the Russians are the major aggressor here? Nine versus 150?"

"Absolutely, the Russians are a major threat to our national security, and we need to be in a position to curtail their aggression," Haverly explained, "our presence in these countries is purely to prevent the expansion of communism."

"But not to enhance the expansion of American influence, then?" Favio asked, "well, it appears to have worked, 150 to 9, I'll give you that but at what cost?" Favio asked.

"I really don't think the American people care about cost, it is the price of our freedom that's at stake here," Haverly said.

"Well, I tend to disagree with you on that point General, I think the American public should be concerned about military spending, especially when the current budget is at 600 billion dollars." Favio gave another pause for the audience to react, "did you know that's as much as the next 10 countries' military budgets combined, including that of Russia." Favio shouted and it prompted more gasps from the audience. "And guess what? China's budget is over three times that of Russia's, they are communist. Why aren't you concerned about the Chinese General?"

"You don't know what you're talking about. The price of freedom is high, you come to this country and spout off these so-called facts, you're lucky you're not locked up." Haverly said, trying to dismiss Favio's facts.

"Funny, I come from a country that wouldn't lock you up for speaking your mind, especially when you are citing facts. That's called freedom of speech, the very foundations of a country you claim you are fighting for. What you're suggesting is exactly the opposite." Favio said smoothly.

"I am suggesting you should be deported, you are defending communism and inciting public opinion against the very values we fought for when we threw you British out 200 years ago." There were a few 'oohs from the crowd as they could sense the General beginning to get a little unhinged.

"Au contraire General, I am saying the complete opposite and I am certainly not supporting communism, I am merely providing you with the facts. Tell me, General, what facts have I stated here tonight that are incorrect? What have I said to you that isn't true and doesn't the first amendment allow me to state these facts?" Favio asked.

"I don't think you have earned the right to quote the American constitution to me," Haverly said.

"I didn't know I had to earn it," Favio said, feigning surprise with his arms outstretched to his sides, "I thought it was an automatic right, for everyone."

"You should think yourself lucky that you can come to this country and say things like this on the air. It is the might of the U.S. who bailed your country out during the second world war, otherwise, you would be under the Nazi jackboot by now," Haverly stated.

"Again General, I have to take exception, I think you should get your historical facts straight," Favio said, "I think it was the might of the Royal Air Force and the Royal Navy that kept the Germans at bay. At the beginning of the war, the Brits were fighting the Axis nations all alone, the Royal Navy was the biggest in the world. Yes, it might surprise you to know that at that time it was far bigger than that of the U.S. and had Britain capitulated the Germans would have seconded that navy, taken Russia, the Middle East and finally, they would have met up with Japan in India. They would have taken the whole of Africa leaving the U.S. and Canada isolated and all alone."

"Isolated, but not beaten, we still had the bomb," Haverly argued, not conceding any ground.

"Really? Remember, there were a large number of allied scientists working on the Manhattan Project that created the bomb. Had Britain been defeated many of those scientists would have been working for the Germans. They may have just beaten the U.S. to the bomb, but there is still another factor you have overlooked. Rockets, the Nazis had rockets that could have been fired from U-boats, battleships or even from the West coast of Africa. What good would isolation have been to you then? Being attacked by Germany on one side, Japan on the other, oh, and let's not forget, the Mexicans from the south. There's no love lost between the Mexicans and the U.S.," Favio said, "without Britain hanging on there would have been no D-day, no second front, and you, my friend, would have also been speaking German or possibly even Japanese by now. Think about that."

"I think you're exaggerating this out of all proportion. The U.S. would never have let that happen," was the best Haverly could reply.

"History tells us differently," Favio said, "President Roosevelt did not want to enter another European war, the consensus of the American public was against it. Meanwhile, the Battle of Britain was raging and at that time, the U.S. was in no position to come to their assistance."

"We just chose what battles we are prepared to engage in," Haverly interjected.

"Yes, just like the type of people you want to let into your country," Favio said.

"You mean like you?" Haverly asked.

"No, I know you would like to see me deported, but while we are on the subject of World War II and rockets, I'm talking of others who were allowed entry into the country. Are you aware that more people died manufacturing the V1 and V2 rockets than were actually killed by them after they were deployed?"

"So? What are you getting at?" Haverly asked.

"It's very simple, Wernher von Braun, the brains behind all the rockets in the NASA program was a Nazi. He designed the V1 and V2 rockets, they were built by slave labor, but was he tried for war crimes? No, instead, he was welcomed here with open arms."

"Simple. He was a scientist and if we didn't bring him to the U.S. the Soviets would have taken him," Haverly said.

"That's a little hypocritical isn't it?" Favio asked, "that's akin to the usual war criminals answer of 'I was just following orders'."

"Then there's another German immigrant, Albert Einstein, yet another top German scientist?" Favio said.

"What about him?" Haverly asked.

"Well, he came to the U.S. in 1933, the same year Hitler came to power. He came to the U.S. as one of the leading scientific brains in the world, maybe of all time, yet it was during a period when even senior members of the U.S. government were against the immigration of Jews, despite the news coming out of Germany as to how they were being treated by the Third

Reich. That attitude continued right up until the beginning of the war. Yet Einstein, even though he was a Jew, was accepted and allowed to stay here," Favio said

"Are you now suggesting that the U.S. was not only hypocritical, but also anti-Semitic?" Haverly asked.

"You tell me!" Favio said. It was at that point the screen faded to black for more commercials.

"On the original broadcast they bickered for a little longer, but you could see the General was seething," Pete explained, "he didn't threaten Fearless but if looks could kill!"

"Darlene, find out where this General Haverly lives and dig into his early days in the military to see what kind of training he had been given," Mario said.

"Got it, boss," Darlene replied as she put down her fork to make a note in her book.

"It is possible a stiletto may have been used," Humph said absently, "that's a favorite weapon of some covert teams. My dear girl, try to ascertain if this Haverly fellow was ever in any special forces, Rangers, Seals, or other units of the ilk."

"Right," Darlene added.

The segment starring General Haverly proved to be the end of the show and they began to finish their refreshments.

"Having seen a few clips of the show I still don't quite understand the hold this Fearless fellow had on people," Humph said, "sure, I understand it was entertaining, if you enjoy watching people be embarrassed and placed in difficult situations. And I appreciate there is a market niche for that type of programming, but was he really that popular?"

"He sure was, he could be very influential," Pete replied, "David told me of one interview that was aired in England that just about destroyed the career of a very popular singer."

"Really? Who was that?" Darlene asked.

"Do you remember Jill Jones?" Pete asked and the others nodded their heads.

"Yet another alliterative name, must be very popular in the media," Humph said to no one in particular.

"Jones had been huge in the '70s and when she came onto Fearless's show a few years ago she was still a megastar. She had this bizarre plan that everyone should give ten percent of their income to charity," Pete began.

"You mean like a tithe to a church?" Humph asked.

"Yes, that's correct," Pete replied.

"Not everyone can afford to give ten percent of their earnings away, they are doing their best to just eke out a living for their family," Darlene responded indignantly.

"Precisely Fearless's point," Pete said, "he reminded his guest of her background, a poor mining village in Wales and he asked her if she ever returned there to help out financially. And here's the rub, she claimed she hadn't spoken to her family in years and since her first number one record she has never returned to her roots. Well, according to David, Fearless just tore into her, apparently, she makes all these demands when she is on tour and has refused to go on stage if something was amiss, a right Diva. Yet she has forgotten her family completely, but still wanted everyone to give to charity whether they could afford it or not."

"So how did the viewing public react to that?" Mario asked.

"Oh, that's not the best part," Pete answered, "do you remember the Christmas song 'Christmas in the Valley'?"

"Sure, that's a beautiful song," Darlene replied.

"Fearless got her talking about the ten percent that she gives to charity, but pointed out that even after providing that much, because of the money she continues to earn and the royalties still rolling in that she wouldn't even feel losing 10 percent like a lot of families on the poverty line, he told her she had forgotten her roots. Then he said that being Christmas time, the show was to be aired Christmas

Eve, she should be more cognizant of that. To which she replied that she didn't believe in Christmas and felt that it was all commercialism. So, he brought up the subject of her Christmas record and she cynically said she was merely capitalizing on commercialism and didn't see anything wrong with that. Fearless pointed out that she earned approximately a half a million dollars each year in royalties on that one record alone. It was played in bars, on the radio, during sitcoms on TV, you would hear it everywhere. Until, that is, after the airing of that show. Sales of her records nose-dived, her concerts had to be canceled due to a lack of ticket sales and you are now hard-pressed to hear 'Christmas in the Valley' or any other Jill Jones record being played anywhere in the U.K."

"Wow, come to think of it, I haven't heard that record lately," Darlene said, "shame, it was one of my favorite Christmas records."

"So, based on that example, it's more than possible that Grover will not escape the opprobrium of the American public after his exposure as a fraud by Fearless!" Humph stated.

"Opprobrium? What the hell is opprobrium?" Darlene asked with a totally quizzical look on her face.

"My dear, it means public disgrace that follows inappropriate conduct as revealed by Fearless on Grover," Hump explained.

"Stick around Darlene, your vocabulary is going to soar working with these guys," Mario joked.

"No kidding," Darlene said.

"Were there other interesting interviews you watched with people who could be considered suspects?" Mario asked Pete.

"Sure, there was an executive with one of the big car manufacturers from Detroit, Fearless went to town with him. Then there was a religious leader from Alabama who got quite belligerent, the heavies came on the set to hold him back."

"What got him so mad?" Darlene asked.

"Fearless mentioned that he was an atheist." Pete replied, "and proceeded to provide reasons for why religion is a delusion conjured up through history by sects in an attempt to control the masses with fear."

"So, it may be necessary to investigate quite a few people regarding their whereabouts," Mario said.

"If we can't come up with something, that is a distinct possibility," Pete replied solemnly, thinking about how much digging that was going to be.

After mulling the various interviews over for a while, the team decided to call it a night. Mario was going to drive everyone home until they figured out that Humph also had his vehicle parked at the morgue and as he lived in the same vicinity of the city as Darlene, he offered to drive her home, while Mario would drive Pete home.

As they were walking out of the bar towards the morgue's car park, Mario told the others about his call with Horowitz and that they shouldn't return to the precinct the following morning. The three detectives agreed to meet in Fearless's apartment early in the morning, Darlene would sweep by the Admin. office to retrieve the printout of accesses and they would resume their investigation from there. As they approached their respective vehicles, they parted company and bid each other goodnight. Mario and Pete were quickly on their way and gave a brief toot on the horn as they left.

"Do you think she will be alright with Humph?" Mario asked.

"Are you kidding?" Pete replied, "Ah, he'll try and flirt with her as he usually does but she's safe enough. I think she can look after herself."

"Guess you're right," Mario answered, "although, I do think he has the hots for her!"

"No question," Pete replied and they both laughed.

There was only one vehicle remaining in the car park and as Darlene and Humph approached it, Darlene stood motionless for a moment in amazement.

"What's the matter? What's wrong?" Humph asked with some concern, he also looked around believing Darlene may have seen some undesirables in the area.

"Is this your truck?" Darlene asked.

"Yes, what's wrong with it?" Humph asked disconsolately, as though his pride had been smitten.

"No, really, I put you down for a BMW or even a Mercedes man, but a truck guy? I would never have guessed it." Darlene replied.

"You don't like trucks?" Humph asked.

"Oh, I love 'em, brought up with them," Darlene replied with a smile, "no, don't misunderstand me, I just wasn't expecting this."

"Only way to travel my dear," Humph explained, "this truck is top of the line, AC, all-wheel drive, GPS, seats five comfortably and I'm sitting above the traffic when I drive, it's perfect."

"But you must use the cargo area for something, surely," Darlene said.

"Sure, during my spare time, which unfortunately I don't get enough of, I like to hike the Appalachian Trail," Humph explained, I'm determined to visit all 2,200 miles of it." Humph unlocked the passenger door and opened it for Darlene to climb into, "so, I can just dump all my camping gear and hiking clothes in the back and take-off."

"Really, I was brought up in Harriman, spent a lot of time on the trail in that area, especially around Bear Mountain State Park," Darlene said enthusiastically as Humph walked around to the driver's side and climbed in.

"Well, interestingly enough, that's one part of the trail I haven't completed yet. Maybe you would like to join me and share with me your knowledge of the area," Humph hinted.

"Would love to," Darlene replied, "but you are aware there have been some violent crimes occurring on that trail over the years, even murders have happened!"

"All the more reason why one of New York's finest should accompany me on future trips, my dear," Humph replied, "yes, I am aware that there are dangers out there, but when you consider how many millions of people are on the trail each year the risk is minimal. Being attacked by a black bear or being infected with tick-borne diseases are just as possible."

Darlene provided Humph with her address and he entered it into the truck's GPS then began to follow the route instructions.

"So, how are you enjoying working with our two intrepid detectives?" Humph asked as he began to drive to Darlene's apartment.

"Hard to say yet, this is my first day with them," Darlene said, scrunching up her face a little in indecision and hesitating, "they seem a little, I don't know."

"Is aloof the word you are looking for?" Humph asked.

"Yes, probably that, but it's almost like they prefer just being by themselves."

"I know what you mean, but don't take it personally," Humph replied, "they're just sounding you out, do your job, you'll be fine."

"I hope you're right because they appear to be a good team," Darlene said almost absently.

"Oh, they are," Humph replied, "by the way, we are very close to my place right now, would you like to come in for a night-cap?"

"Humph, really, it's been a long day and I have to be at the crime-scene in just a few hours," Darlene said with frustration at his attempts to woo her.

"You're right, how inconsiderate of me," Humph replied, "maybe, when the case is solved, as I am sure it will be, perhaps we can do lunch, possibly dinner?"

"Humph, right now I just, want to go home and get a few hours sleep before I get back at it," Darlene said, possibly a little more aggressively than she intended it to be and seeing the dejected look on Humph's face, she added, "but you're right about one thing, this truck is so comfortable and so quiet, I could go to sleep right here."

"Well, don't get too comfortable dear because we are almost at your apartment," Humph said as he turned into the forecourt of her building and parked at the front doors, still appearing to be a little miffed.

Darlene began to gather her things and by the time Humph had stopped, she turned to open the door. Then she hesitated and deftly sidled across the seat to give Humph a quick peck on the cheek.

"Night Humph, thanks for the ride," Darlene said, leaving one happy medical examiner waiting to ensure the new detective on the team entered her building safely.

Friday 18th May 2018

Chapter 11

The following morning, Chief Horowitz arrived in his office, as normal, at 5:30 AM but it wasn't without difficulty. There were already hordes of reporters milling about the precinct's entrance and Horowitz was approached by Seymour, one of the veteran reporters from the Times.

"Any news chief?" Seymour asked.

"Got nothing Seymour," Horowitz answered.

"Any comment on the cause of death?" Seymour said, mining for any gem of information.

"Seymour, if I had anything, I'd tell you. Really, right now I know as much as you do." Horowitz replied as he reached the steps of the precinct. He stormed past the gauntlet of reporters as they all shouted questions at him, some holding out microphones for any semblance of a comment.

As he entered the station, Delaney, another veteran of the force was seated at the front desk.

"It's a zoo out there Chief," Delaney said with a smile, "a bit like the old days."

"Don't say that I've been quite enjoying this quiet new world," Horowitz replied as he continued walking towards his office.

He checked his voicemails, there were three more from the Commissioner. The third call was to remind the chief about how much the TV station had contributed to his campaign and the CEO was now demanding action and expected a speedy resolution to the case.

'Well, I'm sure we will do our best to make that happen,' Horowitz said to himself. He was also taking bets with himself as to what time the Commissioner would make an appearance, he figured about 7:30, he was five minutes off. At 7:35, the lanky, immaculately dressed Commissioner Harper appeared almost from nowhere followed by his entourage of yes-men and note-takers.

"Good morning Chief," Harper said in that perfect Ivy League voice.

"Commissioner," Horowitz replied succinctly.

"I trust you received my voice mails and after listening to them you must realize the gravity of the situation," the Commissioner stated.

"I most certainly did Commissioner and I most certainly do," Horowitz replied matter-of-factly. Harper wasn't exactly the first Commissioner he had dealt with over the years and probably wouldn't be the last.

"So, what do you have for me to tell the press when I leave the building?" The Commissioner asked.

"That our investigations are ongoing, and details will be provided as soon as they become available," Horowitz replied nonchalantly.

"That's it?" The Commissioner answered, he was astonished at the lack of available information. A couple of the hangers-on rolled their eyes in frustration as if the Chief had no idea what he was doing. Needless to say, the Chief merely smiled and ignored them.

"What about the results of the autopsy?" The Commissioner asked, he was gasping for information as though his very life depended on it, "wasn't that carried out last night? Surely the Chief Medical Examiner is aware of the urgency of this case!"

"Indeed he is Commissioner," Horowitz replied calmly, "but until further notice, we want to withhold the results of his findings. We do not want to jeopardize our investigation."

"But surely you can tell me!" The Commissioner said.

"Need to know principle Commissioner. You know how aggressive these reporters can be if I provide you with any snippet of information you may inadvertently let something slip. But if you don't have any facts, the easier it is for you to keep the secret," Horowitz calmly stated as he looked up at the Commissioner from his seated position.

"Secret? What secret?" The Commissioner asked with a puzzled look on his face and leaned forward as if to join the Chief in some kind of conspiracy.

"Wouldn't be a secret if I told you now would it?" Horowitz whispered.

"No, I guess not," the Commissioner replied and straightened up, "continue to keep me up to date," then the Commissioner turned and led his followers through the halls of the precinct and outside to the steps where an even greater horde of reporters was now congregated.

Using a remote, Horowitz turned on the TV that was fixed to the wall of his office, he scrolled down the channel-changer to the news channel showing a live shot of the precinct steps. The caption read, 'AWAITING COMMISSIONER HARPER'S NEWS CONFERENCE' and in the background was the voice of the news presenter broadcasting what few facts they had available on Favio Fearless's demise.

"I understand Commissioner Harper is about to make an appearance, so we will turn it over to our reporter on the spot, Jon Grange," the background reporter said.

"Yes, thank you, Rita, this is Jon Grange, live from the precinct and Commissioner Harper has just arrived and is about to provide a statement," the on-site reporter said, just as Commissioner Harper appeared and began to say a few words into the plethora of microphones that had been arranged on the precinct's steps.

"I have just met with the heads of all the police departments who are investigating the untimely, ruthless attack on Favio Fearless. Believe me, when I say, we have committed all available resources to this case, and we are expecting a speedy resolution. Unfortunately, due to the intricacies of the case, I am not currently at liberty to share with you any of the details, but suffice it to say, the investigation is ongoing. Thank you." On completion of his speech, the Commissioner held up his hands to indicate that there would be no question period and that was the cue for his entourage to lead him down the steps to his chauffeur-driven car that was waiting for him.

In his office, Chief Horowitz merely smiled and switched off the TV and returned to his regular duties.

Chapter 12

In the apartment of Favio Fearless, Mario switched off the TV without making a comment, obviously, the chief had run block on the investigation. Mario had arrived at the apartment with Pete at 6:30 and immediately called his chief with the results of the autopsy. In between mouthfuls of bagel and coffee, he explained what they had learned from the interviews to date and relayed Humph's findings. The chief reiterated his suggestion not to come into the station, he told Mario it was a zoo outside the office. Reporters were hanging around; the phones were ringing off the hook and the Commissioner was in his face because of the chief execs. at the TV station were busting his chops to get closure on the case. Horowitz fully expected the Commissioner to be in the precinct within the hour and that he would be giving a press conference, which is why Mario turned on the TV that was fixed to the wall in the kitchen of Fearless's apartment.

When Mario and Pete had arrived at the apartment building there were a few reporters milling about the esplanade outside, even at that ungodly hour, but the two detectives managed to avoid them. The detectives quickly proceeded to the private elevator and traveled up to the crime scene. Once in the apartment, Pete ensconced himself at the breakfast bar and began to apply a second pair of eyes to the surveillance DVD that Mario had scanned the previous day.

Meanwhile, Mario continued to casually search around the apartment seeking the possibility of ways that someone could have concealed themselves or entered the apartment from anywhere other than the front door.

Just before the Commissioner's press conference came on the air Darlene entered the apartment, smiling and brandishing the list of accesses that Mario instructed her to pick-up the previous night.

"A couple of the Admin. Staff are early starters, they had already printed off the list," Darlene said as she joined the others to watch the Commissioner's press conference.

The three of them watched enthralled at the brief, diplomatic speech given by Commissioner Harper, but before any comment could be made about it, Pete made a simple observation.

"Jeez Darlene, didn't you grab us any coffee on your way in?" Pete asked despondently, which instantly wiped the beautiful smile from Darlene's face and the poor girl looked thoroughly dejected.

"Oh, I get it, I'm the female on the team so I'm expected to wait on you guys is that it?" Darlene said, standing arms akimbo determined not to become a stereotype, "anyway, it looks like you've already had breakfast, and did you think to get me anything?" She pointed to the empty coffee cups and bags.

"No, it's not because you're the female on the team, you were expected to get the coffees because you are the junior member of the team," Mario replied calmly, "and anyway, we drank these coffees an hour ago. Mine's black, Pete's is two sugars and cream." Darlene's mouth was agape as Mario continued to search the apartment while Pete continued to scan the DVDs using the reader, both ambivalent to Darlene's upset demeanor. She was just about to storm out of the apartment when she was given an additional request.

"I'll have a muffin too, please!" Pete added, just before the door slammed behind the departing Darlene.

Surprisingly, it was barely a minute before a smiling Darlene once more opened the apartment door, only this time she was bearing a tray containing two coffees and a plate full of cookies. Mario thought there was no way she could have traveled down to the ground level in that short a time, as she had done the previous day in the precinct. There were substantially more floors and she would have to have found a coffee-shop, ordered and then made it back. Then the reason why she hadn't completed the trip became obvious. Walking into the apartment behind her, carrying two more mugs of coffee, entered Claire. Mario took an involuntary intake of breath at the sight of Claire dressed in another tight-fitting sweater and equally tight jeans.

"I thought you might all be here early this morning, so I had prepared some coffee for you all, just in case you needed some," Claire said, directing her explanation at Mario, much to his delight.

"I thought you only had instant in the apartment?" Mario said, noting by the aroma that the coffee was fresh.

"We did, but after we left great-granny last night my parents and I did a bit of grocery shopping before we returned to the apartment," Claire explained.

"Glad you did." Pete said, reaching for a coffee and a couple of the cookies, "much appreciated."

"How is your great-grandmother?" Darlene asked with sincere compassion.

"Not great," Darlene replied, "the doctors there say we are only talking a few days really."

"Oh, I'm so sorry," Darlene said sincerely.

"Ah, she's had a good long life," Claire said with a sad smile, "it's her time."

"Still, it's never easy is it?" Mario added.

"No, it's not," Claire responded sadly, "well, look, I'd better get back to my parents, we'll be returning to the hospice later this morning," Claire said as she held up her mug of coffee in a cheers gesture, "but if you need anything else, just holler." Again, she directed her comments more to Mario, an action that had not gone unnoticed by either Darlene or Pete.

After the door had closed and a suitable amount of time had passed, Darlene watched as Mario took a couple of sips of his coffee, Darlene decided to get one back.

"You ready for another coffee yet boss?" Darlene asked coyly, "I'm sure Claire would be happy to pour you another!" Pete smiled as he continued to look through the DVDs.

"Darlene, have you scanned through that list yet?" Mario asked belligerently.

"Not yet," Darlene replied, "what exactly am I looking for?"

"You'll know when you see it," was Mario's curt reply, "so the quicker you get on with it the quicker you'll find it."

"On it boss," Darlene acquiesced.

Darlene began to look through the names on the list, wondering how she was supposed to glean anything from it when suddenly, a name did indeed jump out at her like a flashing neon sign.

"Boss," Darlene said fixated on the name on the page.

"What is it?" Mario asked, walking over towards her to read over her shoulder.

"Hutchinson, Daryll, entered the building at 21:55," Darlene whispered.

"Interesting, so, he could have still been here in the building when Fearless returned to his apartment!" Mario said.

Chapter 13

"Pete, go and find our friendly security guard and get him up here, take Darlene with you." Mario told them, "it looks more official if the two of you are together."

"On our way!" Pete responded, and the two detectives left the apartment.

The two detectives returned quickly with a bemused Daryll walking into the apartment between them. Daryll had been standing at the front desk talking to the same two security guys who covered the day shift the previous day. As Daryll entered, Pete and Darlene remained either side of him, Mario turned and faced the man.

"Care to tell us why you returned to the building just before ten, the night Mr. Fearless was murdered?" Mario asked.

"I'd left my cell phone in my locker, I hadn't realized it until that time," Daryll replied.

"What time did you leave work that day Daryll?" Mario asked.

"I told you yesterday, about 5:30 PM," Daryll said after thinking about the question for a few seconds.

"And you felt it was important enough to return to your place of work to retrieve it when you hadn't missed it for almost five hours?" Mario asked.

"Why yes! If there is an emergency at work that's the telephone number the security guards have on file, they will try and call that phone. In fact, that's the only number they have." Daryll explained.

"In the eighteen years you have worked here, how often have you been called in an emergency Daryll?" Pete asked. Daryll thought for a bit and was beginning to shift his weight from one foot to the other in nervousness.

"I don't recall ever being called in an emergency," Daryll said.

"And in the eighteen years you have worked here, how many times have you returned to the building after you have left work Daryll?" Mario immediately asked.

"I can't remember!" Daryll replied, now appearing to be very flustered.

"So, I'll bet never," Mario suggested, "well then, it appears to be one helluva coincidence that on the night just hours prior to Mr. Fearless's murder you re-entered the building at 21:55, having never done this before in all your previous eighteen years of working here."

"I know it seems a little odd, but I can assure you it was pure coincidence," Daryll said in his defense.

"As detectives, we don't like coincidences," Pete said, "and I would have to disagree with you, it is not a little odd, it is extremely odd."

"And of course, conveniently, there is no record of you ever having left the building is there Daryll?" Mario added.

"I left almost immediately after I had arrived, you can ask Fred and Brad," Daryll pleaded, "they saw me come in, I told them why I was there. I went straight to my locker, I knew exactly where I had left my phone, I picked it up and left. I doubt that I was in the building for more than two minutes. On my way out, I waved to Fred and Brad, I even showed them my phone. Ask them!"

"We will, Daryll, we will," Mario said, "but who can verify where you were for the rest of the night?"

"My wife, I arrived home at about 11:00." Daryll offered.

"I'm afraid your wife's testimony is not good enough Daryll," Pete said ominously, "and there's one other thing, at the murder scene yesterday you told Claire Emerson, and I quote, 'it appears that Mr. Fearless has been murdered' when she asked you what was going on, but at that time, you claimed you had not looked at the body. So how did you know he had been murdered?"

"Well, er, I must have heard you mention it," Daryll said.

"I never mentioned it, did you, Mario?" Pete asked as he looked directly into Daryll's eyes.

"No, I certainly didn't. Did you detective?" Pete asked, turning to Darlene.

"Nope," Darlene said succinctly.

"Well, I just assumed, because you were all here and expecting the coroner to arrive that it was a murder, yes that must have been why," Daryll replied.

"Really? Even though we would still have been here if it was a suicide or death by natural causes, the coroner would still have had to have been called." Pete asked, beginning to get a little in Daryll's face, but Daryll chose to remain silent.

"You also told Claire that he had been murdered during the early hours of the morning," Mario said, before adding, "how would you have known that?"

"I didn't know that for certain, I just assumed that because that was when he usually returned to the apartment," Daryll said, but he was beginning to appear decidedly uncomfortable, "look, I didn't have anything to do with his murder. I just came back to get my phone O.K.?" Daryll was beginning to raise his voice. "Sure, I couldn't stand the guy, but I didn't kill him."

"Why didn't you like him Daryll?" Pete asked.

"It wasn't me so much, but he was often rude to Mrs. Emerson," Daryll replied, a little calmer now.

"How was he rude?" Mario asked.

"He would make sarcastic comments about her living in luxury, not knowing how the other half lives, that sort of thing," Daryll replied, "he would threaten that when she died, he would buy the other half of the apartment and rent it out free of charge to homeless people."

"What did she say in reply?" Darlene asked.

"She didn't, she would just ignore him. I wasn't ever here when those conversations took place, she would tell me after the fact, but by then there was never anything I could do about it," Daryll said, "maybe if she had made a formal complaint, we could have looked into it, but she didn't want to make a fuss. She is too nice a person."

There was a silence as Mario turned and walked over to the large, landscape windows. Mario looked out over the city for a few minutes, finally, he turned back to face Daryll and spoke to him once more.

"O.K. Daryll, you can go," Mario said and then added ominously, "for now." Daryll merely nodded his head and turned to leave.

"One last thing," Pete said, "why is there no record of you leaving the building?"

"Nobody touches the keypad to leave the building, you just hit the red button to unlock the exit door," Daryll explained, "there are no records of people leaving the building, just their arrivals, and even then, only after hours."

"I understand that, but as a security guard, wouldn't you have to sign out or something?" Pete asked.

"No, not for a visit like that, if you were here for a few hours, maybe we would log the visit," Daryll replied.

Daryll left the apartment and Darlene held the door open so that the three detectives could watch as Daryll entered the elevator and when the doors closed to dispatch him to the ground floor, they shut the apartment door and began to discuss the interview.

"He didn't do it," Mario said.

"What if he was in cahoots with Mrs. Emerson?" Pete said.

"That's a possibility boss," Darlene suggested, "he certainly has an affinity for her."

"Again, she doesn't have the strength to have used a weapon to kill Fearless," Mario said.

"But Claire does!" Pete said, "and so does Daryll."

Chapter 14

"Claire was in Boston at the time of the murder," Mario replied.

"She claims she was in Boston," Darlene clarified.

"O.K. let's go with that for a minute," Mario said, "let's say they were all in on this, we still have the problem of the surveillance cameras. We still don't have any evidence of anyone entering the apartment or coming out of the elevator or the emergency stairs!"

"Daryll has access to both the surveillance DVDs and the security system, could he have frigged the data?" Darlene asked. The two men looked at her and then at each other, both of them wondering why they hadn't thought of that instead of having a rookie spell it out for them.

"It's possible, he also knows the ropes. He's worked here long enough to know how he could get in and out of this building without being spotted, why would he even have made it so obvious and enter through the front door where it would be recorded?" Mario asked.

"Maybe that's what he had planned, to deflect our investigations away from who really did it!" Pete said.

"Pete, look through those DVDs from about the time just before Fearless got off the elevator, see if you can tell whether the data has been tampered with," Mario said.

"Darlene, corroborate what Daryll said about talking to the guys on the night shift when he came in last night. Call them right now before he can get to them." Mario said.

"Right boss," Darlene replied and immediately began to locate the telephone numbers for the night shift team.

Mario had been just about to call his chief to tell him that at least they had a lead to work with when there was a knock at the door. Darlene was busy on the phone and Pete was checking through the DVDs, so Mario answered the door.

"Hi," Claire said, she was standing in the doorway with that smile that just melted Mario, "how's it going?"

"Er, fine, fine." Mario struggled to reply. One reason was the sheer beautiful sight of her, the other was because she was currently also a target of his investigation.

"Here," Claire said, holding out another tray containing a Thermos carafe of coffee, a small jug of creme, a bowl of sugar, a plate containing some sandwiches and another dish with pieces of cake. As Mario took the offering Claire continued, "this is my mother and father, Angela and Brian Pearson," Claire said, turning to introduce her parents, they merely nodded in greeting, Mario returned in kind. "We're just off to the home so that my parents can spend the rest of the day with great-gran, I will be back later, meanwhile, here's my key to the apartment, if you need anything, go help yourself. I don't quite know what time I'll be back, I have a few errands to run." Claire placed the key on the tray and turned to leave.

"Thanks, thanks very much," was all Mario could stutter as the elevator door opened and the three of them entered into it. Mario's impression was that Claire's parents were not happy about Claire giving up her key to someone that up until the previous day had been a complete stranger.

Pete and Darlene positively salivated when they looked up to see what Mario was bringing into the breakfast nook.

"Don't get used to this detective," Mario said, "we don't normally get the royal treatment at a murder scene."

"Except that donut shop case we were called to," Pete reminded Mario.

"Exception to the rule," Mario replied, as he took Mrs. Emerson's apartment key from the tray that Claire had left and placed it in one of his pants' pocket.

They all grabbed a sandwich, replenished their coffee mugs and continued with their tasks at hand. But not without a few barbs at Mario regarding the attention Claire was giving Mario.

Mario did indeed get around to giving his chief an update on the status of their investigation and as there wasn't much to add, the call didn't take too long. Afterward, Mario called Humph to see if he had any more insights into the killing.

"Nothing but bad news I'm afraid," Humph began, "it is apparent that I will have to retract my suggestion of last night. The fatal wound could not have been caused by a Mogen circumcision clamp inflicted by Friedman. After re-inspecting Fearless's body, I feel that a circumcision clamp would definitely not have satisfied the dimensions of the wound. Furthermore, our other suspect, McCluskey, if he did it, the weapon of choice would not have been a baseball cleat cleaner. For much the same reasons, size, and dimensions just don't fit. Other than that, I am continuing my investigations, but, alas, currently, I have nothing else to offer you."

"Well, never mind Humph, they were both good spur of the moment suggestions and we still can't eliminate either of the suspects," Mario replied, "by the way, how was your trip home with Darlene?"

"Oh, we had a pleasant chat, appears to be a nice young lady. Seems we have a common interest in hiking, she said she would be interested in joining me on a camping trip to Black Bear Mountain," Humph replied enthusiastically.

"Ha, you old dog, never miss a trick do you?" Mario joked.

"I try my boy, I try," Humph replied.

"Well, keep up the good work, catch you later," Mario said and hung up.

The investigation was not going well, Pete had yet to find any anomalies on the surveillance footage. Darlene had just got off the phone after talking with both Brad and Fred, they had confirmed everything that Daryll had told them. So, once more they were back at the starting post with nothing to go on, consequently, Pete returned to the surveillance footage and Darlene began to scan her list once more while Mario did his meandering around the apartment.

As he was moving around the apartment Mario took a final swig of his coffee, emptying the cup, this didn't go unnoticed by Darlene and she decided to get another dig in at Mario.
"Perhaps you want me to go and get Claire to re-fill your cup?" Darlene asked coyly. Pete smiled as he looked at the DVD player.
"Humph tells me you enjoy hiking and camping, he said you were going on a trip with him," Mario retorted, "perhaps we could go on a foursome, you know? You, me, Claire, Humph and yourself. That would be fun, wouldn't it?" Mario didn't have to look at Darlene to realize her cheeks had reddened because Pete was now laughing.

They continued their individual activities in silence for about a further ten minutes until Mario received a call from forensics.
"Harry," Mario answered, "what have you got?"
"Hey Mario," Harry replied cordially, "couple of things. We haven't come up with much from looking through the laptop yet, well, certainly amongst the emails anyway but we're still searching. But I may have something else or I may not, during our search, we checked

out a couple of used glasses that had been found in the dishwasher. They had contained cocktails, we haven't analyzed their contents yet because we were more interested in the fingerprints. Not surprisingly, the prints found on one of the glasses belonged to Fearless, but interestingly enough, the prints on the other glass belonged to a woman and based on our research and the fact that the glasses were still in the dishwasher, I would suggest they were less than two days old."

"Did you run the prints through the database?" Mario asked, hoping they were finally getting a break in the case.

"Yes, we did, and we have a perfect match," Harry replied, "they belong to one Claire Pearson."

Chapter 15

"Did you say, Claire Pearson?" Mario asked as though it was impossible that Claire could have been in Fearless's apartment at any point during the last 48 hours.

"Yes, that's correct, do you know her?" Harry asked.

"She's the great-granddaughter of the neighbor," Mario replied almost robotically, "that's who I was talking with yesterday when I left the apartment, remember?"

"Really? What a coincidence, well, good job we didn't waste our resources trying to track down her whereabouts when you know her already," Harry said.

"That's great Harry," Mario spluttered a reply, not knowing whether he was shocked at Claire's potential involvement with Fearless or excited that they had finally obtained some kind of lead in the case that was worth pursuing. "Thanks for the update, we can take it from here."

"No problem, ciao," Harry replied and hung up.

While Mario was on the phone the mention of Claire's name had caught the attention of both Darlene and Pete. The two detectives looked up from what they were working on, anticipating some ground-breaking news, Darlene quietly walked over to Pete.

"So, what's the story with Harry?" Darlene asked.

"No story, she's just a straight shooter, be honest with her you'll get it straight back at yer!" Pete replied, "her husband is a cop too, Johan DeLuca but everyone calls him Joan. I was at an official function a few years ago, before I teamed up with Mario. The party was to celebrate some old codger's anniversary and Harry and her husband were there. The host introduced the couple to the old guy as Harry and Joan and the poor fellow just couldn't grasp the name gender swap, thought he was going to have an apoplectic fit trying to get his head around it." Pete smiled as he remembered the event.

Mario's call had finished, Darlene and Pete were now both watching Mario, waiting for him to share the latest details.

"It appears that our Miss Pearson had been in this apartment with Fearless at some point on Wednesday, prior to his departure for the studio," Mario explained.

"She didn't even mention that she was in town that day, did she?" Darlene asked.

"No, she didn't," Mario replied slowly. He was leaning against the kitchen counter looking down at the floor trying to evaluate this latest information. "Why didn't she tell us that she was in town that day and why did she not tell us she had been here in this very apartment?" Mario said out loud.

"Which means, she could have remained here in the apartment and waited for Fearless's return that night," Pete suggested, "therefore, she wouldn't have been picked up by the surveillance camera!"

"But she looked genuinely surprised when she was first informed of Fearless's death," Mario said.

"We've seen good acting before boss," Pete countered.

"But what about the phone call she claimed she had made to her great-grandmother from Boston?" Darlene countered.

"There are many ways around that," Pete said, "she could have left her phone in Boston, automated the call or got someone else to call the number."

"What about the surveillance camera?" Darlene suggested, "we could check to see if she had left the apartment that day."

"Good thinking Darlene, why don't you go to the security desk and ask the guards for the DVDs?" Mario told her.

"On it," Darlene replied and left the apartment.

While Mario and Pete were awaiting Darlene's return, they both brainstormed various scenarios based on their latest data. It all depended on, if and when, Claire had left the apartment during that Wednesday. Fortunately, they didn't have to wait long, a breathless Darlene returned, but much to the two detective's surprise she was empty-handed. She looked first at Pete, then at Mario.

"According to our intrepid security guards," Darlene began, "with all the excitement that has been going on, the DVDs from noon until midnight Wednesday have been overwritten and all data for that period is lost."

Chapter 16

"You've got to be kidding me!" Mario said as he pushed himself away from the kitchen counter and ran a hand through his hair in frustration.

"That's one hell of a coincidence, isn't it?" Pete said, "yet another one."

"Don't they back these things up on the cloud nowadays?" Mario asked.

"What they told me boss was that many years ago they upgraded from VHS tapes to the current system," Darlene explained, "but in all the years since then, they have never once been given cause to review the footage. Consequently, the property management company were loathe to invest any money into something that was never required and if something was needed, they thought the current system would be adequate."

"Right!" Mario simply said, "and look where that has left us, critical data could be missing."

"In fairness boss, it is an adequate system, it's the guards that have screwed this up," Pete offered, "human error."

"In the guard's defense, Daryll told me that yes, over the years they had got a little lackadaisical about changing the DVDs," Darlene said, "because no one has ever needed to look at them."

"Maybe there has been more than one person conspiring in this murder after all," Mario suggested. But before he could speculate any more on the subject, the sound of the elevator could be heard emanating through the open doorway of the apartment. Darlene had remained standing in the apartment's doorway and all eyes turned to the foyer as they awaited the arrival of whoever it was in the elevator. They heard the door swish open, a rustle of clothing, then Claire appeared in the doorway of Fearless's apartment.

"Hi, how's it going?" Claire asked casually with a big smile on her face.

You could have heard a pin drop as the three detectives stared at Claire. She must have known something was amiss by the looks they were giving her as she tentatively stepped into the apartment.

"Is something wrong?" Claire asked, "you all look as though you have seen a ghost."

"Come in Claire," Mario said, "please, take a seat."

"I'd love to chat, but unfortunately I have only popped in to pick up a few things for great-gran that I had forgotten to take with me," Claire responded.

"I'm afraid this is important Claire, please, sit down," Mario said with a little more authority this time. Claire sat down demurely without taking her eyes off a stern-looking Mario.

"What's wrong?" Claire whispered.

"We have reason to believe you were not only in New York earlier in the day before Mr. Fearless was murdered, but you were also in this very apartment with the victim," Mario said. Expecting to hear a flurry of denials, Mario was extremely surprised to hear her acquiescence to the question.

"Yes, that's correct," Claire responded, still looking confused and concerned about the line of questioning.

"Why didn't you tell me that when I interviewed you yesterday?" Mario asked with an officious tone in his voice.

"You didn't ask!" Claire replied very offhandedly.

"Didn't you think to tell me that you being here on the day before Mr. Fearless was murdered was somehow relevant?" Mario continued in the same tone.

"No, no I didn't," Claire replied in kind, "you asked me where I was at the time of Favio's murder, which I told you, I was in Boston. Am I supposed to give you my complete schedule for the last ten years?"

"No, but I would have thought it would have occurred to you that your whereabouts only hours before the murder would have been relevant, especially when you had been in the victim's apartment," Mario replied indignantly.

"Well, that's because you're a detective, I'm not," Claire said defiantly.

"What were you doing here with Mr. Fearless?" Pete asked the question that he knew Mario wanted to ask, but was probably having a problem asking, afraid of what that answer might be.

"I'm not sure that is any of your business," Claire replied.

"This is a murder investigation, Miss Pearson, that makes it our business because we need to obtain a complete picture of exactly what went on during the time leading up to the murder," Darlene explained gently.

"Well, if you must know, I came to inform Mr. Fearless that my great-gran would be moving out of her apartment and that she will probably never return," Claire replied in a soft voice.

"But I didn't think there was any love lost between your great-gran and Mr. Fearless," Mario said.

"There's not," Claire responded, "but that doesn't mean we can't maintain a civil relationship. After all, we are the only two occupants on this floor. I thought it was only proper that he should be told his only neighbor is dying and won't be around much longer. Is that too much to expect?"

"No, it isn't," Mario replied humbly, "but I'm trying to establish everyone's whereabouts prior to the murder. It is important that I do that, any little thing could have a bearing on the case."

"Ah, so you're now considering me a murder suspect, are you?" Claire responded indignantly, but then continued in a more conversational fashion, "well, if you must know, after explaining the situation to Favio he invited me in for a drink, which under the circumstances, I gladly accepted, I needed one. He was very sympathetic and offered not only his condolences, but also his assistance whenever he could. He'd lit a couple of those scented candles to provide a calming atmosphere," Claire nodded in the direction of the kitchen unit where three candles were set in an expensive solid silver, candelabra, "after the hectic few days I'd had, I found it all extremely relaxing and very welcoming."

"From what we know of Mr. Fearless, especially when it came to your great-grandmother, wasn't this friendly approach a little against the grain?" Pete asked.

"Yes, it was, but I thought it very becoming of him," Claire said.

"After the drink, what happened then?" Mario asked.

"What do you mean, what happened then?" Claire asked askance, looking directly at Mario with those beautiful eyes wide open, "what do you think happened, I took the drink, we chatted for a while and then I left."

"Can you remember the time period you were here Miss Pearson; specifically, what time was it when you left this apartment?" Darlene asked.

"It would have been just after noon when I arrived and I couldn't have been here for more than fifteen minutes," Claire replied, "I remember because I wanted to get back to help prepare great-gran's lunch before I left for my flight to Boston, which I am sure you can verify, AX 122 out of LaGuardia, my name will be on the passenger manifesto. Now, is that all?"

"Yes, I think that has explained everything," Mario reluctantly replied. He was a little disturbed for many reasons, not least of which was that their brief relationship had now taken a sour turn. This was endorsed when Claire made a big deal of gathering up her tray of coffee things, including the uneaten sandwiches and cookies, much to Pete's chagrin. Although, Mario found it strange that she forgot to ask for her apartment key to be returned.

"Oh, Claire -" Mario got as far as saying before he was cut off by a look from Claire that could have stopped a truck.

"It's Miss Pearson if you don't mind!" Claire hissed.

"Pardon me, Miss Pearson, forensics found a comparison of your prints in their database; how would there be a record?" Mario asked, thinking she had at one point been charged with a misdemeanor or some other crime that could be relevant to the case.

"If you must know, I had a summer co-op job working for the Coastguard. I had seriously considered it as a full-time career but unfortunately, I never really overcame bouts of sea-sickness, so after my first term completed, I never returned. It was during that period my fingerprints were taken for a security background check. I'm surprised you hadn't picked up on that detective." Claire said with a pompous air, then she turned quickly on her heel and departed.

After Claire had left, the three detectives said nothing, Mario was looking down at the carpet, despondent that a potential relationship had now simply dissipated. They heard Claire's apartment door slam and Darlene walked over to Fearless's apartment door and made sure that it too was closed.

"Well boss, what do you think?" Darlene asked.

"I don't, I think she's clean," Mario replied.

"I don't know boss," Pete chipped in, "it could have been anyone on that plane saying they were Claire Pearson and as I mentioned earlier, that late evening phone call is also a weak alibi. She could have been in this apartment when Fearless left for the studio and remained here until his return."

"What time did she leave?" Mario asked, "has there been any sign of her at any point on the DVD footage."

"We haven't checked before or beyond the approximate time of the murder," Pete countered, "she could have left at any time up until the discovery of the body."

"Darlene, go and get the DVDs from the time of the murder until David arrived and discovered the body," Mario ordered, but Darlene remained leaning against the front door with a very sheepish look.

"Sorry boss," Darlene said quietly, "the security guys also informed me that they don't have any valid DVDs beyond the one that Pete has over there. That one takes us up to about noon when they get changed. More relevantly, when they got screwed up."

"You've got to be kidding me!" Mario said once more.

"'Fraid so boss," Darlene said, "a major clusterfuck."

"Are you getting the same feeling as I am?" Pete asked, "I'm telling you, I think there is more than one person involved in this."

"I'm not so sure," Mario replied, "this isn't the first time we have encountered sloppy security guards and the mishandling of surveillance camera data."

"True," Pete agreed, "but this is beginning to look creepy to me."

"So, let me get this straight," Darlene began to talk out loud as she paced the room. She was attempting to clarify what they had just learned, "Claire was in this apartment prior to Fearless leaving for the studio, we have no proof that she ever left except her say so. This means, she could have remained here and when Fearless returned, committed the murder, then stayed holed up in this apartment until after noon when the DVD changed. Then she could have left, safe in the knowledge that somehow, the DVDs that showed her comings and goings would be screwed up! Sounds damn fishy to me."

"You've got that right!" Pete agreed.

"Let me chew on that for a bit," Mario said, "but meanwhile, let's get back to what we were doing. Pete, that means reviewing the DVD that we have got and Darlene, you continue looking through that list of key-code entries for anything suspicious.

For the next hour, Mario walked around the apartment trying to evaluate all the data they had to date. Although there were potential scenarios, there was nothing of real substance, nothing seemed to be gelling together, then Darlene gave out a loud shout.

"Eureka. Guess what?" Darlene asked excitedly.

"Go on!" Mario said.

"Dexter Haverly is a resident in this building," Darlene said.

Chapter 17

"Get out! You mean the same General Haverly from the interviews?" Mario asked.

"You're kidding?" Pete said, "how do you know it's the same guy?" Pete asked.

"I don't for certain, but how many Dexter Haverlys can there be?" Darlene asked.

"Find out which apartment he's in!" Mario said.

"I've got it right here on the printout, apartment 404," Darlene said.

"Let's go," Mario responded as he grabbed his jacket and began putting it on as he headed for the door.

"I'll stay and carry on reviewing this DVD," Pete said.

On the elevator down to the foyer, Darlene gave Mario an update on a couple of the tasks he had assigned to her the night before in the bar.

"It looks like our Jewish friend, Friedman, has been out of the country all week," Darlene said as she flipped through her notebook, studying her notes, "apparently he was at some retreat in Israel, it had been planned for weeks, way before he knew about the interview with Fearless."

"Well, I think, based on that and Humph's findings we can safely eliminate him from our inquiries," Mario said.

"I also spoke briefly with David the producer," Darlene continued to read through her notes, "he doesn't recall ever talking to our baseball player, McCluskey, and is pretty sure nobody else said much to him either, apparently he was very aloof and arrogant around the crew. After the interview, McCluskey stormed straight out of the studio. As for his whereabouts, the Mets sent him down to their triple-A club in Las Vegas immediately after their game with the Blue Jays. Apparently, he went straight to the airport after the game to get out of town."

"Wow, so that's another one we can safely rule out." Mario said, "our suspects are disappearing rapidly."

"Also, I received a printout of Fearless's telephone calls from the telephone company," Darlene added, "I carried out a quick scan of Fearless's telephone usage, all the local calls were for service companies, food delivery, travel agencies and the such, but interestingly there were quite a few for the same number out in California which I will be following up."

"Good work Darlene," Mario replied.

By now, they had reached the foyer and they transferred to another bank of elevators, the ones used by all the other occupants of the building. The elevator that was available was empty, so Darlene continued with her update as they entered, and she pressed the button for the fourth floor.

"As discussed, I haven't bothered obtaining any details of our Vietnam vet., Grover; and I have yet to find out anything about Haverly's training and background," Darlene said.

"Well, hopefully, we're probably about to find out about him!" Mario said as the elevator stopped, and the door opened onto the fourth floor.

They followed the arrow pointing to the even-numbered apartments and arrived at what they hoped would be their General Haverly. Darlene rang the doorbell. The door opened and indeed, standing there was the very same person they had seen on the television program the evening before, except they were both surprised by the stature of the man. He was, in fact, a big man, a good 6' 2" Mario thought and about 200 pounds with very little body fat. The image of him on television did not do justice to the physique of the man and Mario was beginning to regret not being accompanied by Pete, this fellow looked intimidating. He had close-cropped hair, as per army types, his dark eyes looked cold, but alert and his lips were thin giving him a very sardonic look. He was dressed smartly in slacks and wore a color-coordinated golf shirt.

"Who are you?" Haverly asked in a deep, gruff voice that portrayed an intolerance for incompetence.

"Detective Mario Simpson, NYPD and this is Detective Darlene Knight, can you spare us some of your valuable time please?" Mario asked as he held out his badge for the General to see.

"This is about Mr. Fearless, isn't it? You think I did it don't you?" Haverly asked.

"We would just like to eliminate you from our inquires General Haverly," Mario stated calmly.

"Well, I had nothing to do with it, although I am not surprised, the little shit had it coming to him," Haverly said as he stood back, opened the door and beckoned them in.

Mario and Darlene entered the apartment, it was neat, and the walls were all covered with military paraphernalia including several stilettos, daggers, guns, and rifles. The apartment even had a faint smell of gun-oil and boot polish. Judging by the lighter color of the paint on the wall Darlene noticed that there was one spot where obviously something used to be hanging there but was no longer. There were photographs of the general at various stages during his military service and even a couple with Presidents Clinton and Bush. He had obviously had a distinguished career. There were also a few photographs of an Asian lady and what appeared to be her children during various stages of their lives.

"Can I offer you anything, coffee, water, something stronger?" Haverly asked cordially.

"Thank you, no," Mario said.

"Sit," Haverly said politely, indicating a comfortable looking sofa while he plonked himself down in a well-worn armchair that was positioned by the window.

"We'll get straight to the point General Haverly," Mario began, "where were you on the night of Wednesday 16th May until the early hours of the following morning?"

"I went out for dinner, had a couple of drinks with some old army buddies and got back here at about 9:45 in the evening," Haverly replied. Darlene looked down at her list, to verify the time captured during Haverly's pass-key usage, it was a couple of minutes out but close enough.

"Can anyone verify that?" Mario asked.

"Regarding where I was up until I arrived home, yes, I can give you names, but I live alone, so no, I cannot give you any alibis after my arrival here," Haverly replied. There was a silence as both Mario and Darlene stared at the General.

"So, you have nobody who can verify your whereabouts from 9:45 onwards during the night in question?" Darlene asked, sounding all official.

"Are you suggesting that I killed Fearless?" Haverly asked, "that's absurd, I didn't even know he lived in this apartment building until I saw all the emergency vehicles turn up here after his murder."

"Excuse me! You didn't know he lived in this building?" Darlene asked incredulously.

"Why would I? It's a big building, I hardly ever see people on my floor, let alone those from other floors. We're all like ships in the night. For all I know we could have other celebrities living here, I would never know," Haverly explained calmly. "Hell, he even used a separate elevator to the one I use."

"Surely maintenance staff or the security guards say things," Mario asked.

"I rarely talk to any of the people you mentioned, not because I consider myself above them, I don't. I merely use this apartment as a base, I travel from place to place from here, in and out. The only time I interface with staff is when I need to, and then it is generally by telephone." Haverly explained.

"So, you're telling us that you had no idea Fearless lived in this very building," Mario asked.

"Affirmative," Haverly replied.

"What kind of military training have you had during your career General?" Mario asked.

"I was in some elite forces, and yes, before you ask, I have been trained in hand-to-hand combat and worked on many covert operations. So I am certainly capable of killing your Mr. Fearless but I wouldn't waste my time." Haverly said.

"But you had a motive," Darlene said, "he embarrassed you during your interview with him."

"Embarrassed me? It would take a lot more than that little jumped up limy to upset me," Haverly said in disgust.

"General, I couldn't help but notice that there's a vacant spot up there on your wall. What used to be hanging there?" Darlene asked. Mario immediately looked to the wall as though an object had suddenly disappeared before his very eyes, but he didn't let on he was both surprised and impressed by Darlene's acute observation.

"Oh, that," Haverly said, laughing, "it was a knife I had on one of my very first sorties back in the day. It had gotten so rusty and was falling apart, I just felt I should remove it from view, it looked unruly."

"What type of knife was it?" Darlene pressed him.

"A stiletto," Haverly replied.

"Do you still have the knife?" Darlene asked.

"No, despite the sentiment, it was time to throw it away," Haverly said, but then asked, "is that the type of weapon that was used to murder Fearless?"

"Investigations are ongoing, no weapon of any kind remained on the scene, but the indication is that it could have been a stiletto," Darlene replied.

"Well, I can assure you it wasn't mine," Haverly replied.

"You keep the place very tidy General, it must be your military training," Darlene said abstractedly.

"Thank you, but I am too busy to do the cleaning, so I have someone come in to do the cleaning every other day," Haverly explained, "her name is Anne."

Chapter 18

Mario and Darlene quickly looked at each other in total surprise. That name again, 'Anne', the same cleaner that Fearless employed. Haverly must have sensed he had struck a nerve telling them about his cleaner.

"I believe she has other clients in this building. Now, unless there's anything else, I have places to be." Haverly stood.

"General, we may have more questions, I must ask you not to leave town until our investigation is complete," Mario said.

"No, I'm not going anywhere, and you know where I live," Haverly said as he escorted his guests to the door.

"Good day," Haverly said as his guests were in the corridor and then he shut the door, leaving the two detectives looking at each other, decidedly unsure of the guilt of the man and that of the one person they hadn't yet interviewed, Anne.

Nothing was said between them, but the fact was, they both thought the same thing, as a suspect, Haverly was a definite maybe and they also had to get hold of Anne, she had suddenly become a person of interest in their case. As they walked back to the bank of elevators, they couldn't discuss the interview because they had to side-step an old man placing a couple of refuse bags down the garbage chute. However, during the two elevator rides back to the late Fearless's apartment the two detectives discussed their findings.

"I don't like it, detective," Mario said, "continue to check out Haverly's background. He obviously has the skills and a reason for killing Fearless but how the hell could he have got into the apartment without being detected by the cameras?"

"Not forgetting the missing stiletto," Darlene said, "remember Humph said that's the type of weapon that could have been used, that's one hell of a coincidence."

"No kidding!" Mario agreed. "I'm surprised he even fessed up to it."

"Couldn't really deny it, the shape of the discoloration on the wall was too obvious," Darlene explained.

"Right," Mario replied, then thought for a bit before continuing, "now, Darlene, you also have to get hold of this Anne woman and oh, by the way, there's one other thing I thought of, check out Daryll's background. He said he started working here in '92 but what was he doing before that?"

"On it boss," Darlene replied, making a note of the requests, just as the door swished open onto the penthouse suites.

"How goes it, Pete?" Mario asked as they entered the apartment.

"Nada," Pete replied dejectedly, "if this DVD was doctored, it was carried out by an expert and it would take forensics to determine any tampering because I sure as hell can't. How did you make out with the General?"

"Suspicious," Mario said.

"One wall was filled with weapons and there was a small gap where a stiletto once hung," Dalene explained, "the General said he threw it away, it was rusty. Oh yeah, and he doesn't have an alibi for the time of the murder." Pete's eyebrows rose a little.

"So, you think he's a suspect?" Pete asked.

"Absolutely," Mario replied, "if only we could figure out how he got into this apartment without being seen."

"But that's not all," Darlene added, "guess who is also the General's cleaner?"

"Anne?" Pete guessed, "this is beginning to smell a little fishy!"

"Yes, but it's a matter of hanging it all together, all we have is little snippets with no substance," Mario said, "it's finding that glue that binds all these little facts together, that's the crux of this case."

"Well, for a start, I'm going to copy these DVDs onto my laptop and email them to forensics right now, maybe they can come up with something!" Pete said and he began to do just that.

"While Pete's doing that Darlene, find out where this Anne is, she maybe somewhere in the building with all these clients she supposedly has. If she's not here, find out where she lives, then begin to investigate the backgrounds of Daryll and the General." Mario instructed the overwhelmed newbie detective. Which left Mario at a loose end, so he decided he needed some quiet time to think things through, so, despite the changed circumstances under which Claire had lent him the key, he opted to enter the solitude of Mrs. Emerson's apartment.

As he entered the apartment one more time, he couldn't help but think it was like going back a little in time. Coming from Fearless's apartment, with all its modern decor, spaciousness and light to enter these darker rooms with its fifty's furniture cluttered with knick-knacks from a lifetime of collecting. He strolled through the rooms with idle curiosity, trying to clear his mind while looking at the variety of objects littering the tops of shelves, sideboards, and the various tables. On the walls were numerous photographs, mainly of old Mr. Emerson, but there were also many of what appeared to be a young Edgar Emerson. One picture especially stood out, it was a large portrait of Edgar in full military uniform and was the centerpiece on one wall of the apartment.

Mario continued his mind-clearing by entering into the crafts room once more, marveling at the various stained-glass creations and the number of sophisticated tools that dominated part of the wall above a bench, complete with a vice. He noticed objects of all shapes and sizes that had obviously been used to shape various craft type creations. There was even an old cigar container, the one that he noticed was missing from the rack the previous evening. A workboard was standing upright on the wall, it was scoured with solder, cuts, holes, paint, and glue, amongst other substances that he couldn't identify. Mrs. Emerson had been one busy lady during her life-time.

Mario decided he had lingered long enough, he turned and walked out of the craft room and out of the apartment. He ensured he had closed the door behind him and returned to the crime scene.

"Feeling better?" Pete asked, knowing full well of his boss's idiosyncrasies.

"Not sure, you can't swing a cat in there without hitting something, it is so cluttered with stuff," Mario said.

"Swing a cat?" Darlene said, looking up from her laptop, "that's a pretty cruel thing to say isn't it?"

"It's just an expression Darlene!" Pete admonished her.

"Yes, but it's the sort of politically incorrect expression that needs to be eradicated in this day and age. I had a cat, I find it distasteful." Darlene replied in disgust.

"Darlene, it doesn't refer to a real cat, it refers to the cat-o-nine-tails that was used on ships to dish out punishment, a kind of whip." Pete explained, "it's an old British naval expression," Pete said, "ergo, they needed room to swing the 'cat'." Darlene still looked a little bemused.

"How do you know this shit?" Darlene asked, once more exasperated at Pete's unseemly infinite knowledge of useless information.

"I'm half British, I told you that yesterday, my mother always came out with old expressions like that," Pete replied.

"Now I know what it refers to I'm not sure whether I prefer the other explanation. Either way, they both sound cruel to me." Darlene said, returning to her research.

"It's a cruel world!" Pete said.

For the next hour, Pete continued to laboriously scan the DVD for some hidden clue that had been missed and Darlene investigated the backgrounds of their suspects. Meanwhile, Mario kept pacing around the apartment, sometimes into the foyer to see if a spark of wisdom would help him solve the murderer's modus operandi. His best explanation continued to be that someone had tampered with the DVD, obliterating any evidence of an intruder, but that line of investigation was beginning to grow thin. His thoughts were interrupted by the sound of the elevator emitting through the open door of the apartment. When the door opened Daryll exited, accompanied by a tall, slim, attractive, young man that bore a striking resemblance to Claire.

Chapter 19

"Hi detective," said Daryll, "this is Claire's brother, Michael, he's just flown in from San Francisco."

"Hi Michael," Mario said as he held out his hand to greet the man. Michael took it and they shook hands. Mario instantly realized why Michael lived in San Francisco. The pressure of the man's hand-shake was weak and soft, his clothes, although not flamingly flamboyant, were nevertheless effeminate. Not that Mario was homophobic, it was merely an observation and he understood perfectly the reason for someone leaving the pressures of a city like New York and its foibles when you could live a less inhibited life on the west coast.

"Yes, Michael has come to gather a few things to take to the hospice but as you hadn't met him yet, I felt it was best he should talk to you first," Daryll explained.

"Thanks, Daryll," Mario said, "but really, I only have one question, I need to know where you were on the night of the 18th."

"I was at home in San Francisco. I received a call from Claire saying that great-gran was being moved to the hospice and it wouldn't be long before...." Michael began to say, but he brought his hand up to his mouth to stifle a sob and attempt to stem the tears that were beginning to well up in his eyes.

"It's O.K., Michael," Mario said quietly, tapping him on the shoulder in an act of consolation, "I'm sorry but I had to ask." Michael merely nodded his head in agreement and then without another word he walked over to the apartment and using his key, entered and shut the door behind him. Daryll, compressed his lips as if he understood, nodded to Mario and without a word returned to the ground floor via the elevator. Mario stood there for a few seconds, processing this new data, but decided to almost eliminate Michael from his thoughts and list of suspects.

After Mario re-entered Fearless's apartment, he explained the details of his meeting with Michael to the others.

"Pete, just a thought, when you reviewed the segments of Fearless's interviews were there ever any instances of gay-bashing?" Mario asked.

"I think you mean homophobia," Darlene said.

"Negative, although I could check with Dave the producer," Pete said, completely ignoring Darlene's politically correct comment.

"Yeah do that, but I think that will be a dead-end," Mario replied absently.

About ten minutes later, Pete confirmed that homophobia, for whatever reason, was one area that Fearless had never pursued, Darlene lifted one arm in an act of triumph and whispered an almost inaudible 'yes' as she had succeeded in having them use the correct term.

Approximately thirty minutes later, with Pete intently staring at the DVDs and Mario muttering and shaking his head as he continued to pace around the apartment the silence was suddenly interrupted by another cry from Darlene.

"Wow. Guess what?" Darlene said and turned to face the two detectives with a look of absolute triumph. "I have been reviewing a timeline of General Haverly's army career. What is significant is that he was one of the first soldiers to be inducted into the U.S. Army Delta Force when it was founded in 1977. He was a Major when his unit was sent to Grenada in 1983, but here's the kicker, guess who else was also in his unit?" Darlene asked.

"O.K., hit me!" Mario said.

"Private First Class Daryll Hutchinson," Darlene replied.

Chapter 20

"The plot thickens," Pete said.

"No kidding," Darlene said.

"But didn't Haverly tell us that 'I rarely talk to any of the people' when we asked him about the people who work here?" Mario asked.

"Yes, he did," Darlene confirmed as she flipped through her notes.

"I find it difficult to believe that when you have served in a small unit during a real live invasion that you can completely ignore someone who had been a member of your team; when you see them years later!" Mario said.

"You don't!" Pete said.

"But there's more!" Darlene, said, reading the data being displayed on her computer screen, "our boy Daryll was raised just outside Albany, New York. From a young age he loved climbing in the Adirondacks, he was an expert rock climber, one of the attributes that got him into Delta Force and why he was selected for the Grenada unit."

"The elevator, it has a maintenance door on the top that can't be opened from the inside, but if you had the appropriate key, which I'm sure Daryll would have access to, he could have entered the elevator shaft, climbed on top of the elevator, jumped down, then murdered Fearless before climbing back up into the shaft and making his escape, unseen," Pete suggested.

"But the body was in the apartment!" Darlene said. "I don't understand."

"That was a bonus," Pete suggested, "what if the original intention was to leave the body in the elevator, the discovery would still not have been made until David came to check on his star. Nobody else uses that elevator with Mrs. Emerson in her state of health. As it happened, Fearless, being the stubborn bastard that he was, in his death throes still managed to make it to his apartment before finally dying. That has made the murder even more mysterious."

"Possible and we can't rule it out, but Humph has already said that it was extremely unlikely that Fearless could have accomplished that after receiving the fatal blow," Mario replied.

"O.K. so what about this scenario, it's not beyond the realm of possibility that when our man Daryll returned that evening he could have fooled the guards into thinking he had left the building, then quietly went up to the roof, abseiled down and gained access into the apartment through the balcony door, where he waited for Fearless's return home. After the deed was done, he climbed back up to the roof and left the building without being seen." Pete suggested.

"Abseiled? What the hell is that?" Mario asked.

"It's descending a rock face or in this case, the apartment wall by utilizing a doubled rope coiled around the body. The rope would be fixed at a higher point, in this case, the roof," Pete explained.

"How do you know this shit, Pete?" Darlene asked.

"Summer camp when I was a kid, believe it or not!" Pete replied with a quick hunch of his shoulders as though everyone knew what the expression meant.

"We need to check the roof to see what structure a rope could be tied to and get forensics to scan it to see if there are any fibers up there," Mario said.

"They probably have window cleaning apparatus up there too that could have been utilized," Pete suggested.

"Check it out, but talking about Grenada, didn't Fearless bring up that invasion during his interview with Haverly?" Pete asked.

"Yes, he did, he may have just struck a nerve there," Mario said.

"And what about the knife that was missing from Haverly's wall?" Darlene added, "the two of them could have been in this together. Shouldn't we get back up there to confront Haverly about this, and then bring Daryll in again, only this time really grill him. When he returned to the building the other night he could have climbed up to the roof and entered the apartment through the balcony door to lie in wait."

"So, do you think it is possible that Daryll scaled the outside wall somehow and came in from there to lie in wait for Fearless's return home." Darlene mused.

"We still have the problem of entry into the apartment, I can't see how he managed to gain entry through that balcony door," Mario replied, pointing to the balcony door. "It's locked from the inside and the track suggests that the door hasn't been opened for some time."

"He could have made it look as though it hasn't been opened for some time." Darlene proposed, "remember, Daryll could have unlocked the door days ago while Fearless was at the studio, who would have noticed? After killing Fearless, he could have left the way he came, with the knife," Darlene added, "he was also the first security guard on the scene, although he claims he didn't touch anything I doubt whether David would have noticed if Daryll slipped in to lock the balcony door and at some point sprinkled dirt onto the track to make it look as though it hadn't been used." Mario looked at Darlene with a tilt of his head as he was weighing up that possibility.

"It's a good thought, but that dust on the track appears to me to have been there for some considerable time," Mario said as he was walking over to the garbage chute with a wrapper from one of the cookies that Claire had brought in earlier. Suddenly, a new option struck him like a thunderbolt.

"Pete, come here and take a look at this chute," Mario said to his sidekick. Pete got up from his chair and walked over to the garbage chute that Mario was holding open.

"It just occurred to me that on all the other floors there is a shared garbage chute used by all the clients. But for the two apartments on this floor, they were installed right in the kitchen area. Do you think it is possible someone gained access through here?" Mario asked as he was trying to peer deep into the dark access of the chute.

"It's about 18 inches wide, tight fit, but not impossible." Pete said as he inspected the orifice, "the only issue I would have with that suggestion is that the perpetrator would have been scraping against the side of the chute, like a human flue brush. On emerging from the chute, the perp. would have been covered in all sorts of crap, let alone stinking to high heaven. If someone had climbed up through here, they would have to clean themselves off before setting foot outside this kitchen area," Pete looked down at the clean, expensively tiled Terra Cotta floor, "otherwise forensics would have had a field day with all the rubbish on the carpet."

"Don't they clean these chutes on a regular basis?" Mario asked, "and anyway, after the murder occurred, whoever did it, would have had plenty of time to remove any evidence. Once the perpetrator had cleaned up, he could then have exited back down the chute," Mario said.

"Or she," Darlene quickly added.

"To quote you boss, possible but very improbable," Pete replied.

"Daryll could have done it. He knows the building and with his military background a chute wouldn't have been too daunting for him, but could he have fit into that?" Darlene asked, looking at the garbage-chute door Mario still held open."

"Hey, we have a dog-door at home for our pooch, it leads out to the backyard. On more than one occasion I have had to contort myself through it because we had locked ourselves out and it's way smaller than this." Pete told them, "yeah, I think it's a possibility that Daryll could have climbed up into this area from a lower floor."

"I agree and I also think there's a link between Haverly and Daryll!" Darlene offered.

"O.K. we need to talk to them both again. Darlene let's go!" Mario said, then looking at Pete, "work with forensics to try and dig up something from those DVDs. O.K., Pete?"

"No problem," Pete replied, returning to his assigned chair to continue to look at the DVD reader.

As Mario and Darlene descended in the penthouse elevator once more, neither of them said anything as they were both consumed with the various possibilities that had just been discussed. On reaching the ground floor Mario couldn't see Daryll hanging around the security desk, so before they went to the other bank of elevators to ride up to Haverly's apartment, Mario had a couple of questions to ask the security guards. As Mario and Darlene approached the men at their desk, they were greeted with a smile.

"Quick question for you, do you know when the garbage chute was last cleaned and disinfected?" Mario asked.

"Sure, it was last Thursday. We have a company come in once a month. They do a good job," one of the guards replied. Mario and Darlene looked at each other, it certainly gave credence to the chute theory. After all, how much garbage would Fearless have thrown down the chute in the few days between the last cleaning and his murder?

"Great, thanks," Mario replied, "oh, one other thing, I don't see Daryll around, we need to discuss something with him. We are just going up to visit another guest so when you see him, please mention that we have a couple of questions for him. Could you tell him to stop by Fearless's apartment when he can please?" But this time the guard's reply caught Mario and Darlene completely off-guard.

"Oh, you've just missed him, he's gone to the hospice with General Haverly to visit with Mrs. Emerson. Her daughter doesn't think the poor old lady has much longer left so they both wanted to pay their last respects before she, well, you know!"

Chapter 21

The guard's response to the question regarding Daryll and Haverly's whereabouts hit Mario like a thunderbolt, but he tried his best not to show any signs of surprise and carried on as though everything was in order.

"One more thing while we are here. There's a cleaner who works in the building for a few of the clients, her name is Anne, can you tell me if she is in the building right now?" Mario asked.

"Anne? Apparently, she is not in today, she was so upset after learning of Mr. Fearless's murder our understanding is that she had to go to the doctor to get some tranquilizers. Don't know when she will be back," the security guard told Mario.

"Do you have an address for her, where she can be reached?" Darlene asked.

"No, she is not employed by our property management company, she just works freelance for some of the occupants of the building. As such, we have no details about her. She doesn't fall under our jurisdiction." The security guard then hunched his shoulders in that expressive way to say he neither knew about her nor cared.

"Do you know the clients she has in the building, maybe I can get contact details from one of them?" Darlene asked.

"My understanding is that she only looks after General Haverly in 404 and the two apartments in the Penthouse suites," the security guard replied.

"That's it?" Darlene asked, surprised, "I thought she had numerous clients in the building."

"No, just those three as far as I know," the security guard said.

Mario and Darlene immediately returned to the apartment and explained the latest developments to Pete.

"The plot gets even thicker," Pete remarked, "I can understand Daryll wanting to pay his respects to Mrs. Emerson, but why Haverly?"

"Precisely!" Mario replied, "so now there seems to be a connection between Haverly, Hutchinson, and Emerson in addition to Haverly, Fearless and Emerson."

"We need to find this Anne woman," Pete said, "she could be the key to unlocking this case."

"Great, but right now, the only people who we know that know anything about her are all at the hospice or are dead," Mario replied.

Pete was going to say something, but was interrupted by another shout from Darlene.

"Got it!" Darlene had gone straight to her laptop on returning from the ground floor and while Mario was telling Pete about Daryll the

General and Anne, she had at least hit upon the connection with Mrs. Emerson and the General.

"Vietnam, it was the General's first tour of duty and he served in the same unit as Edgar Emerson," Darlene explained.

"It is looking more and more like somehow, they were all in this together," Pete submitted to Mario.

"But it gets even scarier," Darlene added, "Haverly was also in Iraq in '93. Wasn't that when Fearless was stationed there?"

"Jeez, so they could have met then and maybe something went down as far ago as that!" Pete said.

"Let's not jump to conclusions here," Mario said, trying to keep everything on an even keel, "there's no indication that Fearless and Haverly's paths ever crossed in Iraq, that's just pure coincidence."

"But there's no indication they didn't!" Pete countered, "yet another coincidence."

"O.K. let's go with that for a minute. Two of the suspects have served in the same theatre of war together and there's a link between them and another war involving one of the suspects and another suspect's son. What I still can't figure out is why they would risk murdering someone just because one of them had been verbally attacked. And in the very building, they live or work. It doesn't make sense," Mario replied, "they would have to know they would be prime suspects."

"Maybe they had succumbed to the biggest mistake all murderers make, they thought they had come up with the perfect murder and they wouldn't get caught. Let's be realistic, we have potential murder suspects, but not one scrap of evidence to implicate any of them," Darlene said with some pessimism. Both Mario and Pete looked at her with disdain, if looks could kill.

"Darlene, we haven't been on this case 24 hours yet, we'll find something, that's why it's called 'an ongoing investigation'." Mario admonished her, "and if that is going to be your attitude you can go back to the station right now! Is that enough evidence for you?"

"Sorry boss, my bad," Darlene said demurely, returning to look back at her laptop keyboard.

"Let's just slow down and take stock of what data we have got here?" Mario said to no one in particular. "Let's take a look at all of our suspects individually."

"Boss, Fearless has a whiteboard in his den why don't we use that?" Darlene asked.

"Good thinking Darlene," Mario said as he picked up his cold coffee and led the others into Fearless's den. The den was furnished with comfortable, easy chairs, poufs, an expensive bureau housing a laptop and a printer. There was also another 60-inch smart TV and a state-of-the-art total surround audio system. Darlene went straight to the board and wrote 'Mrs. Emerson' on it using a black marker that was on a tray affixed to the board. Underneath that name, she wrote 'Claire Pearson' followed by all the other names of the people currently under suspicion.

"O.K., Mrs. Emerson, what can we say about her?" Darlene asked as she stood beside the board awaiting comments from the two men. Darlene had become the self-appointed scribe and there didn't seem to be any argument from the other two who were sitting back in the easy chairs. "What are the Pros and cons?"

"Let's say Fearless was attacked with a weapon, there's no way Emerson could have done that," Mario said, "could she have fired something? Possible, but wouldn't we have detected that on the surveillance DVD. Also, where's the bullet or whatever it was that killed Fearless? It had to have been removed. It is extremely unlikely that Mrs. Emerson could have removed an object from Fearless's lifeless body and anyway, there's no sign of her moving between apartments."

"Does she even have a motive?" Pete asked.

"Other than she didn't like the man I don't know of one," Mario replied.

"What about Claire?" Darlene asked. Pointing to the next suspect on the list.

"Again, a motive may be an issue, furthermore, she says she was in Boston at the time of the murder and we have no proof she returned to the building," Mario said.

"Not impossible to get from Boston to here and what if she crept in when Fred went out for air," Darlene suggested.

"Or he let her in," Pete suggested, "what if he was in on it?"

"We still have the same problem with Claire as the murderer for the actual attack. Yes, she is probably strong enough to administer the fatal blow, but if we go with the scenario that Fred let her in, she would still have appeared on the surveillance camera. Either when she left the elevator at the penthouse or after carrying out the deed, but she's not on it!" Mario countered. "Unless, of course, we return to the 'stay in the apartment' scenario. Maybe we should add Fred and Brad to your list of suspects on the board." Darlene proceeded to add their names to the list.

For a few seconds, the three of them considered those scenarios before Darlene moved on to Daryll.

"Motive unknown," Mario said.

"But more than capable of carrying out the attack," Darlene said.

"He could have climbed down from the top of the building, he would not have shown up on the surveillance cameras. We also know he was in the building a few hours prior to the time of the murder." Pete stated.

I still don't believe anyone came in through that balcony door," Mario said, "that door hasn't been unlocked for some time."

"What about the theory that Fearless's assailant rode up in the elevator with him and did the deed there?" Darlene asked, "that assailant could have been Daryll or someone let in by Fred."

"Doubtful, you heard what Humph said, the fateful blow was probably instantaneous," Mario replied.

"There's still the theory of the garbage chute," Pete said.

"I think forensics would have picked up on an inordinate amount of garbage found in the kitchen area," Mario suggested.

"Not necessarily, if Daryll or whoever used overalls and took them off in the kitchen. There would be no trace on the carpet," Pete suggested, "as we said earlier, how much garbage would Fearless have thrown down that chute since it had been cleaned out? Any traces of garbage found on the floor would have belonged to Fearless anyway. They may not have considered any garbage findings in the kitchen an issue."

"He has a point there, boss," Darlene said.

Mario thought about that and conceded that there was nothing wrong with the scenario, but his gut just wouldn't buy into it. "I can't rule Daryll out, but I can't get the surveillance footage out of my head. There's something there and all I can think of is maybe all the security guards are in on this and they have somehow frigged the

DVDs." Mario said. "What if they destroyed the original DVDs of the night of the murder and replaced them with DVDs from another night and somehow frigged the dates and times. Let's face it, I bet you dollars to donuts they have a number of DVDs with Fearless entering the floor with his coat and briefcase at approximately the same time every night."

Darlene looked at Pete, it was a possibility that had not been considered.

"So, we're returning to the theory that they could all be in on it or at least a combination of them," Darlene said.

"Then, of course, there is the unknown factor, our cleaner Anne," Mario suggested, "every scenario that we have contrived with Daryll, the General and Claire can equally be true for Anne. We have clear surveillance footage of her entering Mrs. Emerson's apartment just before noon on the day before Fearless was killed and we have no idea when she left because of the DVD screw-up.

"So, she could have remained in Mrs. Emerson's apartment and done the deed when Fearless came home, then left after the DVD changeover!" Darlene suggested.

"Which would have meant that both Mrs. Emerson and Claire were complicit in the murder because Anne never turned up to make lunch," Pete said

"Or maybe she wasn't scheduled to that day," Darlene offered, "remember Claire said that when she was here in the apartment with Fearless, she had to return to prepare her great-granny's lunch."

"That's right, she did," Pete said, "and it would also mean one or more of the security guards was involved in the murder to screw up the appropriate DVDs."

"But there's still the problem of the weapon used," Mario said, his voice laced with frustration.

"What about the balcony angle?" Darlene asked, "could Anne have somehow used that as a means to gain access by crossing the roof and coming in through Fearless's balcony, as we thought Daryll may have done?"

"No, Fearless's balcony hasn't been opened, I'm sure of it" Mario replied, "no I'm beginning to think that the fact that Anne cleaned for all of these people is purely coincidental."

"But what about Haverly?" Darlene asked, "he denied knowing that Fearless lived in this building, yet he knew the only other occupant on this floor, Mrs. Emerson, and they shared the same cleaner. I find it difficult to believe he wasn't aware of Fearless living here."

"Me too, but again, we have no proof that he knew nor of his involvement in the crime," Mario replied, "again, just coincidences, I believe we are making this far too difficult for ourselves, we're overthinking it."

"But that's just it boss, there are far too many coincidences in this case, just look at them all," Pete said and began to count down on his fingers all the potential suspicious acts together with a commentary, "one, Anne has a doctor's appointment and conveniently had the morning off on the day of Fearless's murder. Two, Anne just also happens to be the cleaner for Fearless, Haverly and Mrs. Emerson and no one else and has keys to the apartments. No one is aware of her address or where she has been for the last two days. Three, Daryll returned to the building the night of the murder, never in all the years he has worked here had he ever done that before. Four, Fred leaves the building a short time before the murder, possibly allowing an opportunity for a perpetrator to enter the building, maybe even Claire. Five, the DVDs prior to and after the murder are all screwed up. Six, Haverly and Daryll served together during covert operations. Seven, Haverly served with Mrs. Emerson's son in Vietnam. Eight, a stiletto used to hang on the wall of Haverly's apartment, but has conveniently been thrown out, and what was the weapon that could have been used for this murder? A stiletto. Nine, Claire just happened to be in this apartment prior to Fearless's murder when she claims she had never been in this apartment before. Ten, Haverly and Fearless were stationed in Iraq at the same time as each other. Boss, we're lucky to uncover one coincidence on a case, here we have ten."

"I agree, it is suspicious and it's certainly possible they are all, or a combination of them are in on it but somehow I can't get my head around it. In isolation, there's still nothing tangible in any of those suppositions," Mario replied slowly.

"There's still one other suspect we haven't considered," Darlene said slowly.

"And who's that?" Mario asked.

"David, the producer guy!" Darlene replied.

"Nah," Pete said, "I confirmed with the guy he gave a lift home, the times checked out."

"He could have been lying," Darlene said.

"True, but do you honestly think David has the stature to have inflicted that wound in Fearless's chest?" Pete asked, "what's more, I don't think he has the balls to carry out such an act let alone have a motive, he owes his career to Fearless."

"But he does have a key to the apartment," Darlene added.

"Yes, he does, but unless he hid in Fearless's briefcase there is no way he could have entered the building undetected," Pete said.

Suddenly, at the mention of the briefcase Mario's attention was drawn to it. The briefcase that Fearless had been carrying when he had entered the apartment at the time of his murder had been placed on one of the plush settees, presumably by forensics. Mario pointed to it, "has anyone checked the contents of Fearless's briefcase yet?"

"I think Harry checked through it, but I haven't," Pete replied and then he looked over at Darlene who was shaking her head.

"Maybe Anne had packed his lunch," Darlene said.

Mario walked over to the briefcase and undid the buckles on the straps. He lifted back the flap and inside were a number of folders, each one had a tab with a hand-written name on it. Flipping through them with his fingers he could see that each name represented interviewees, most of the names were of people who had already appeared on the program, but the folder that caught Mario's attention was of someone who had not yet been interviewed on television, that name was Emerson.

Chapter 22

"Lookee what we have here!" Mario said as he slowly extracted the folder from the briefcase and held it up to show the others. "Favio Fearless had composed a file on the Emersons." Mario looked through the folder, inside were small stapled dossiers on each of the Emerson clan; Brian and Angela Pearson, Michael, Claire, Mrs. Emerson, Ralph Emerson, and Edgar.

"Here Pete read through these two," Mario said and handed Brian and Angela's files to Pete.

"Couple for you Darlene," Mario said and passed the papers for Michael and the late Mr. Emerson to Darlene. He kept the files of Mrs. Emerson, Claire, and Edgar to read through for himself.

Each of the three detectives selected a comfortable reading chair and began to pore through the documentation. After about fifteen minutes or so, Mario had finished reading two of his papers and looked up to see how the other two detectives were faring, they were both almost done. Mario waited another couple of minutes, then began talking.

"Well, there was nothing worth talking about in the two files I managed to get through," Mario said, "pretty mundane actually."

"Can't say the same for Mr. Emerson," Darlene said, "it appears the man was a bit of a philanderer. He got caught up in numerous affairs and even had a couple of children out of wedlock. Lawyers were involved and it looks like the matters were settled out of court, but at some cost."

"Are any of the other family members aware of his discretions?" Mario asked.

"According to what we have here, they are not aware of the settlements, which could also explain why he was almost bankrupt. These were pretty hefty sums he had to pay out to buy these women's silence," Darlene explained, "as for the affairs, you've got to think his wife knew what was going on."

"Maybe not, he was in insurance sales, remember? Evening appointments were the norm in those days," Pete suggested, "she just thought he was out working his little buns off, which of course he was."

"Do you have to be so crude?" Darlene admonished him.

"What about Michael?" Mario asked, trying to keep the investigation on track.

"Nothing much really," Darlene said, flipping through the pages, "yes he was part of the gay community here in New York before moving out west but nothing Fearless could get his teeth into."

"What about you Pete?" Mario asked.

"Mr. Pearson is a bit of a bust, nothing too exciting but Mrs. Pearson, now that's a different story," Pete replied. "Before she met her husband, she liked to party in her younger days, clubs, discos and she was even into heavy drugs. She got busted a couple of times but here's the interesting bit. According to the notes written here, she also had two abortions, results of affairs with two different guys, both of whom were public figures, although it doesn't say here who they were."

"Interesting," Mario said.

"Oh, I haven't finished yet!" Pete said with a smile, "our Mrs. Pearson has also been having a long-running affair with one Daryll Hutchinson."

Chapter 23

"Very interesting," Mario said.

"You think Fearless was preparing to do a 'tell-all' on the Emerson family on the air?" Darlene asked.

"I'm not sure whether there is enough substance to make a program out of what he has here," Pete said, tapping on the folder, "although he may have been using the information for leverage."

"You mean blackmail?" Darlene asked.

"Possibly," Pete replied.

"Unless, he was still working on finding out who the public figures were that Mrs. Pearson had the affairs with and the subsequent abortions," Mario said.

"Maybe Mrs. Pearson got wind of this dossier and decided to shut Fearless up once and for all!" Darlene said.

"But she and her husband were on their way up from Florida at the time of the murder," Mario said.

"They say," Pete countered, "they could have already been in the city. Here's something else for you to consider," Pete continued, "what if Claire's visit to this apartment was not to talk about Mrs. Emerson's move to a home at all, but to discuss Fearless's investigation into her family."

Mario sat back on the settee where he had chosen to carry out his reading and just looked up at the ceiling.

"So, we're back to all or any one of them having a vested interest in murdering Fearless," Mario said.

"It certainly looks that way to me," Pete agreed, Darlene nodded her head in agreement too. Mario continued to mull it all over before speaking.

"O.K., let's say for a minute they were all in on it, we still have no idea how the murder was carried out and by whom!" Mario said, getting more frustrated by the minute.

"By the way, you haven't mentioned what was in Edgar's file," Pete said.

"No, I didn't get to it, here, you take a look," Mario said and tossed the folder to Pete.

"So, this Anne seems to be a will-of-the wisp type," Darlene said, "she had a key to all of her clients' apartments, she could have flitted from apartment to apartment and nobody would have thought twice about it."

"You're right, but the same could be true of a host of other cleaners or service personnel who operate in the building," Mario countered.

"But, as Pete said, having Haverly, Fearless and Mrs. Emerson as her only clients, isn't that a little too much of a coincidence?" Darlene asked.

"There may be a simple explanation for it and until we interview her, we won't know what that common thread is," Mario explained.

"Oh my God!" Pete suddenly shouted out, "Edgar's marriage to his wife, Avril, was a shotgun affair, a quick registrar wedding," Pete said.

"So that's why she took off after Edgar died and left the baby with the Emersons to bring up," Darlene said.

"No, no, I don't think that was the reason at all," Pete said with a big smile on his face, "on his tour of duty Edgar fell in love with a young Vietnamese girl and she was pregnant with his child at the time he was killed."

"Can this get any more complicated?" Mario said.

"Yes, it can," Pete said, enjoying every minute of this, "Haverly was responsible for sponsoring the girl to come to America. Her daughter was born in the States, her name is 'Hang'."

Chapter 24

"'Hang', what kind of a name is that?" Darlene asked, her face was all screwed up as though the sound of the name was so horrible.

"It's a lovely name, it means moon in Vietnamese," Pete explained.

"Jeez, how do you know this shit?" Darlene said as she rolled her eyes and looked up at the ceiling.

"One of my uncles was in Nam, he was good with languages, he learned to speak the lingo," Pete said, "we used to talk a lot."

"Hang on, excuse the pun, but wouldn't that make Hang an heiress to Mrs. Emerson and subsequently, a challenger for Mrs. Pearson, so if this information got out that could upset the apple cart, couldn't it?" Darlene asked.

"Not necessarily, Angela would still be the eldest, she would have to be because Avril was pregnant with her before Edgar went to Vietnam, which is why they had to get married. In this day and age, I don't think the situation would be considered scandalous, but still, I don't think it is information that they would like to see plastered all over the airwaves." Mario explained.

"What intrigues me is how Fearless got hold of all this information," Darlene said, holding up the dossiers in her hand.

"I wouldn't mind betting it was from Edgar's estranged wife, Avril, and she wouldn't have done it for free. In fact, I wouldn't be surprised if she had approached Fearless with the smut and him being a good investigative reporter, he did the rest," Mario speculated as he tapped the dossiers he had sitting on his lap. "Even so, I'm not sure any of this is significant as to who murdered Fearless."

"Not significant?" Pete was astounded by his boss's indifference to this latest information, "what about Haverly's involvement?"

"What about it?" Mario hunched his shoulders and compressed his lips, "it was some fifty years ago, just an act of friendship on Haverly's part that's all."

"It seems to me that anyone of this group, or a combination thereof, could have been involved in this murder. Either by firing something at Fearless from the Emerson's apartment or being in this apartment and attacking him with a sharp object." Pete suggested, "then tampering with the CDs to remove all evidence of a weapon and movements of perpetrators."

"I hear what you are saying Pete, but I think we are over-complicating the problem. I find it difficult to believe that more than one of the people we have interviewed is mixed up in this." Mario said.

"But we haven't interviewed Anne yet and she had a key to this apartment," Darlene reminded Mario.

"She did, but I don't believe she is a suspect," Mario said, then in a moment of sudden inspiration, he looked at the DVD reader that was still out on the breakfast nook, "I still maintain the key to this murder is on that DVD, I'm certain of it."

"But I've studied them for hours boss, forensics have had them for what?" Pete said, as he looked at his watch, "a couple of hours now, and nada."

"Did you check specifically the dates and times?" Mario asked.

"No, not specifically, but I think I would have still noticed any tampering," Pete said in defense "and if they have been tampered with, I don't think Daryll or any of the other security guards have the necessary expertise to frig around with these DVDs to the point that I can't notice any interference."

"I respect what you're telling me Pete, but we're missing something on those DVDs. I don't know what it is, but we have to find it." Mario stressed. Mario rose and led his team towards the DVD reader that remained in the kitchen area.

"Pete, bring up the screenshot just before Fearless gets off the elevator and let's all study it and take it from there."

"Why don't I attach this reader to the TV in the den, so we can all see it more clearly?" Pete asked.

"You can do that?" Mario asked.

"Yes, I can do that," Pete replied with some frustration at his boss's total lack of technological understanding. Pete carried the reader to the comfort of the den and began to attach cables to the TV and reader. He turned on the 60-inch TV, changed a couple of settings and the Penthouse portal that was being displayed on the reader appeared on the TV in all its HD glory. The three of them each selected a comfortable armchair as the DVD began to play. The three of them gazed intently at the screen for what seemed an interminable age, but in fact, it was only a couple of minutes before the rear of Favio Fearless's head appeared on the large TV as he exited the elevator. As he walked toward his apartment the rest of his body came into full view, then he stopped to put his key into the lock, he opened the door and entered his apartment. Once more there was nothing to see but the empty foyer of the two penthouse suites.

"He doesn't seem to be walking with any discomfort, does he?" Mario said.

"Not to me," Pete agreed, and Darlene merely shook her head.

"I think we can rule out a hitch-hiker on the elevator then!" Mario said quietly as he continued to watch the TV. After a few seconds of watching an empty penthouse foyer, Mario spoke up once more.

"Did any of you see any glitch that would indicate the dates and times had somehow been manipulated?" Mario asked while still gazing forward at the TV?" Pete and Darlene replied simultaneously with 'No'.

"O.K., Pete one more time, but as soon as Fearless's head comes into view, can you slow it down?"

"Sure can," Pete replied.

Once more Fearless's head appeared, and Pete slowed down the speed of the footage. All three of them were searching in vain for some semblance of a clue that could help them in their investigations. The film showed Fearless entering the apartment, then disappearing from view, Pete waited for a few seconds and then reached forward to press the stop button on the reader.

"Wait, what was that?" Mario shouted out, "play it back, play it back!" Pete went back a couple of tracks, but neither he no Darlene could see what it was that Mario could see.

"There, right there!" Mario stood up and walked over to the TV to point to what it was he could see, Pete immediately stopped the player. There, being displayed on the TV was a barely, visible, transparent, object of some kind.

"Oh, that?" Pete said, "it's just a rod."

"A rod?" Darlene asked, "what the hell is a rod?"

"When you look at old photographs and films you can see these rods that appear to be shooting across them. One conspiracy theory is that these rods are actually UFOs. There is evidence to support such a theory, this being a potential example," Pete pointed to the now static screen, "photographic and video images that capture strange rods flying through the air."

"Are you now suggesting the murder was committed by a UFO?" Mario asked askance.

"No," Pete laughed, "you asked what rods are and I'm just telling you. Another plausible theory is that the rod is possibly an insect that got captured on the film, giving the impression of a rod, as we may have here. Although this is obviously a digital image, a lot of the older photos probably had faults in the photo-paper, or a problem was caused during the development process which created the rod."

"So, if this is digital photography, what caused the rod?" Mario asked.

"As I said, it could be an insect, a glitch who knows?" Pete replied.

"How do you know this shit, Pete?" Mario asked.

"You just have to search for 'flying rods' on the internet," Pete replied casually, "you'll bring up loads of sites, I thought it was common knowledge!"

"Never heard of them, I think you have way too much time on your hands Pete," Darlene replied, shaking her head sympathetically.

"O.K. Play it again at normal speed, I want to identify this flying object," Mario asked Pete. Pete did as he was asked, and the few seconds of footage were replayed. At normal speed, the rod, as Pete had called it, was so quick that it was not discernible to the naked eye.

"Once more at reduced speed," Mario instructed. Again, Pete complied and after the clip had completed, they all stared at the screen for a few seconds.

"O.K. once more, but this time, stop it so we can study your rod, I think we may have something here," Mario said enthusiastically. Pete obliged and halted the footage to reveal the rod.

"Is there any way you can zoom in on the rod?" Mario asked.

"Sure!" Pete replied, he tapped a couple of buttons on the reader and the object on the screen was magnified 10 times.

"See," Pete said, holding out an open palm, it appears to be transparent, it's just a blip. Boss, one of these days I will have to bring you into the 21st century, so you can set things up like this all by yourself."

That last remark twigged something in Mario's memory and he suddenly looked directly at Pete. Mario held his gaze for a few seconds, then he looked back at the screen and squinted his eyes somewhat at the rod, not so much to view the object any clearer, but more to work out the embryo of a theory that was beginning to form in his head.

"What did I say?" Pete questioned his boss, "I know that look, you're onto something aren't you boss?"

"Pete, get forensics to identify the dimensions of your so-called flying rod, I want size, speed and trajectory, I just have to go and make a couple of calls," Mario said.

"Have you cracked it, boss?" Darlene said, trying a little flattery to get back into Mario's good books.

"Well, to quote your academy vernacular Darlene," Mario began, "we've known the what, when and where for almost 24 hours, but now I also think I know the who, why and how."

"How can you tell who did it from that rod?" Darlene asked, "if it was a projectile, where is it? It's not in the body! What happened to it because there is no evidence of anyone removing the weapon?"

"To quote a famous detective, albeit a fictional one, 'when you have eliminated the impossible, whatever remains, however improbable, must be the truth.'"

Chapter 25

As requested, Pete contacted forensics with his boss's questions while Mario returned to the Emerson's apartment. Mario had claimed he wanted some additional quiet time while he made his calls. After about an hour of seclusion, Mario reappeared and listened intently as Pete gave him the updates from forensics.

"I think we need to take a little trip to the hospice, hopefully, the whole gang will still all be there," Mario said.

"Will we need back up?" Darlene asked, anticipating a problem if multiple arrests were to be made.

"No, we will be able to handle this all by ourselves," Mario replied as he began to lead the way to the elevator.

"Could we stop to grab something to eat on the way?" Pete asked, "it's been a long while since we had those sandwiches this morning, I'm starving!"

"Sure!" Mario replied, rolling his eyes.

Pete drove to the hospice via one of his favorite burger joints, one of the many that he knows scattered across the city. Darlene was excited about going to an arrest in her first homicide case. She sat in the front seat beside Pete with Mario seated in the back. She began pumping Mario with questions, but Pete, well aware that his boss was still thinking through the facts he placed a hand on Darlene's arm to catch her attention. Darlene looked at Pete as though she was about to be admonished, but Pete had a smile on his face and he merely wanted to shush her with the questions, which he did by holding his forefinger to his lips. Like Pete, Darlene said no more for the remainder of the trip.

Although it was Pete who had insisted on stopping to grab a bite to eat, the others didn't waste the opportunity, they both bought something too. They ate on the go and arrived at the hospice where they provided their credentials at reception and were escorted to Mrs. Emerson's private room by the head nurse. The hospice had been converted from what appeared to have once been a mansion and there were many private rooms leading off from the central corridor they were walking along. Everything about the place was old, the floor tiles, ceiling and skirting boards but they all appeared immaculately clean and infused with that antiseptic odor that always seemed to hit you in medical establishments. They arrived at Mrs. Emerson's room and the nurse knocked gently on the door, it was slowly opened by Claire whose expression turned to one of total surprise when she saw who the visitors were. It was a big cumbersome hospital door and it had to be opened quite a distance, but once open it revealed the whole Emerson family. In addition to Daryll and the General being present in the room, there was also Brad and Fred, paying a visit to Mrs. Emerson just before they started their shift. There was also a tall, attractive Eurasian woman with short dark hair standing at the head of the bed holding a glass of water for Mrs. Emerson. The woman's eyes were red and puffy as though she had been crying for some considerable time. She would have been approximately the same age as Mrs. Pearson, Pete was about to ask who she was and what she was doing there, but Mario placed a restraining hand on Pete's arm and whispered to him, shielding what he was saying to him by bringing his other hand across his mouth, "unless I'm mistaken, that woman is Anne and I fully expected her to be here." Standing next to her was a man and a woman approximately the same ages as Claire and Michael, Mario assumed those were Anne's children.

The occupants of the room stood in a horseshoe pattern around the bed with the old Mrs. Emerson lying at the open end. What was significant was the positioning of everyone, on one side of the bed, stood the Pearson family and on the other, Anne, her children, Brad, Fred, Daryll and the General who was standing nearest to Mario. At the sight of the three detectives, Haverly immediately marched purposely towards them as they stood in the doorway.

"Look here, the Emersons may be too polite to tell you, but this is a totally inappropriate place and time for your inquiries," the General blurted out, "have you no shame?"

"Detective, I know you have a job to do, but surely, whatever it is you want, isn't this something that can wait until we are back at the apartment?" Claire said, almost pleading with Mario.

"I'm afraid not, this is the only place and time," Mario replied gently, but with some authority.

"No, I'm, sorry, this is unacceptable, I'm afraid you will have to leave. This is distressing for all concerned, especially for my wife's grandmother," Mr. Pearson now entered into the discussion. It was the first time Mario had heard him speak, it was a high-pitched voice that certainly belied his tall frame. Meanwhile, Mrs. Pearson was consoling a distressful Michael, Daryll merely looked on, happy to let his superior officer handle the flack. The perturbed looks on Brad and Fred's faces indicated that they would rather not be there at all. Through all this, Eleanor Emerson lay motionless, watching the proceedings with clear alert eyes and a slight smile on her lips.

"Let them be," Mrs. Emerson said with a quiet voice that was almost inaudible above the noise of the oxygen coursing through the tubes that traveled into her nostrils. Everyone looked at her, the matriarch had spoken, so they slowly and reluctantly returned to the positions they had adopted prior to the intrusion. Pete closed the door to the room and Mario walked towards the bottom of the bed while Pete and Darlene remained like sentries by the closed door, as much in the dark as to what Mario was about to say as the other people in the room. The room went silent and Mario now had the attention of everyone in the room, it was then that he delivered his bombshell.

"Mrs. Eleanor Emerson, I'm charging you with the murder of Ivan Anderson aka Favio Fearless."

Chapter 26

Everyone in the room began to shout at once, but above the cacophony of sound Claire's voice was the most vocal.

"You can't be serious!" Claire shouted at him, but Mario ignored her protestations and continued to read Mrs. Emerson her rights.

The initial reaction to Mario's accusation had now dissipated and everyone's mouths were agape except for Mario's and the elder Mrs. Emerson's, even Pete and Darlene were taken aback, they did give each other a quick glance, showing total surprise, although they did their best not to display any emotion to the others.

"Have you lost your mind? How could she have possibly killed a big strong man like Fearless, she can hardly stand?" Mrs. Pearson wailed.

"I must admit, that baffled me for a while until I happened to be in your apartment Mrs. Emerson and all the facts were right there," Mario stated.

"What facts?" Mr. Pearson asked.

"It was a roll of ribbon that Claire had retrieved from the floor on my first visit to the craft room and the upturned work board standing against the wall that started me thinking. The board was randomly pierced with splintered holes with shards of wood all over the workbench. I thought, why would a neat, tidy fastidious woman like Mrs. Emerson leave splinters of wood scattered over her otherwise neatly arranged workbench? Then, carelessly leave a roll of ribbon on the floor where it would be an obstruction to her means of access which was a walker or a wheelchair? So, I placed the roll of ribbon back on the floor where Claire had found it. Turns out that it was exactly 20 feet from the doorway of the room to the upturned work board. Which, coincidentally, is exactly the same distance between the door of your apartment and that of Mr. Fearless's." Mario explained, looking directly at Mrs. Emerson, "isn't that correct, Mrs. Emerson?"

"That's exactly all it is detective, a coincidence," the General said.

"Detective, do you have a warrant to search through my great-grandmother's apartment?" Claire demanded.

"No, I don't," Mario replied.

"Then you had no right to go searching through her apartment and all your evidence would be ruled irrelevant in a court of law!" Claire stated. "I know enough about the law to know that much."

"Then you will also know enough about the law to know, that what you say is not so. I don't need a warrant," Mario replied, "as you recall, you left me the key to the apartment and invited me to go and help myself to anything I needed." Mario reached into his trouser pocket and held up the apartment key to substantiate his claim.

"Regardless," Claire said, trying to dismiss the semantics, "what does anything you have said prove that my great-grandmother killed Mr. Fearless?"

"Mrs. Emerson practiced firing bolts from a crossbow in her craft room. She accomplished that by unrolling a short, strip of ribbon and placed it on the floor to be used as a distance marker, then aimed for the work board, hence the holes." Mario said.

"That's preposterous!" The General said, laughing, "are you mad? She doesn't have the strength to load a weapon of that kind, I know, I've been trained in them. She would never be able to load a crossbow with the poundage necessary to kill a man."

"The modern crossbow is very light and as for the loading, Mrs. Emerson used a crank, a simple device to wind back the bow-string, load the bolt and fire. Isn't that right Mrs. Emerson?" Mario asked, but the elderly lady said nothing and just returned his gaze with that slight mocking smile on her face.

"This is ridiculous," Claire said with some vehemence, "if that is what she did, where is the crossbow, where are the bolts?"

"Oh, they're long gone. Mrs. Emerson disposed of them down the garbage chute." Mario calmly replied, "Mrs. Emerson knows only too well the timing of the garbage trucks. The crossbow is easily assembled and disassembled, a simple bolt is removed, separating the head from the stock and the entire apparatus could easily be disposed of. By the time the body was discovered, the garbage could have been anywhere."

"But what about the bolts?" Daryll asked, "my understanding is that no weapon has been found. How could Mrs. Emerson possibly have retrieved the bolt? She would have been caught on camera."

"That too left us guessing, for a while," Mario said, continuing to look directly at Mrs. Emerson. "But Mrs. Emerson is an extremely gifted lady when it comes to making things so when it came to the manufacture of a crossbow bolt that would magically disappear that became no problem at all did it, Mrs. Emerson? So, you came up with a way of making a bolt made of ice. You used one of the old cigar tubes left by your husband as a mold to manufacture the bolts. The tube left in your craft room still had a few drops of condensation trapped inside it. You filled the tube with water, left it in the freezer and once you had extracted the frozen bolt from its casing you shaved the rounded end to a point. On the night of the murder, you had the door of your apartment slightly ajar and you were in your wheelchair with the crossbow cocked waiting for the sound of the elevator to alert you of Mr. Fearless's return to his apartment. Once you heard that familiar sound of the elevator coming up the shaft you reached for a bolt from the freezer and loaded the crossbow. You waited for Fearless to exit the elevator, open his door and it was at that moment you called to him. When he turned, you fired, he fell backward, and his door closed behind him. That was the only potential bugbear in the plan wasn't it, Mrs. Emerson? Had Fearless had fallen into the corridor or blocked the door with his body, he would have eventually been seen by the security team monitoring the cameras and you would have been caught out, not that you care, under the circumstances. But fortunately for you, it all went according to plan and the force of the bolt knocked Fearless backward and his door automatically closed behind him, concealing the body. Between the initial body heat of the late Mr. Fearless and the sun shining into the apartment for most of the day, the ice bolt melted so that by the time the first person arrived on the scene there was no trace of what had killed Mr. Fearless. Meanwhile, you had disposed of the weapon down the garbage chute and the spare bolts, they could have easily been placed in the sink and left to melt. Then, you just waited for the fireworks to begin, hoping you would have passed away before the murder could be solved, if it ever would."

"My god, how crass can you be, detective?" The General asked, "I'm going to make sure your superiors hear about this, everything you are saying here is pure conjecture, so far I haven't heard you mention a single scrap of proof."

"He's right, you're just guessing, you're so desperate to close this case you've come up with a contrived story to accuse a 90-year-old lady, knowing full well she will be dead in a couple of days," Claire said angrily, and that drew another uncontrollable sob from Michael.

"And your case will be closed without anyone contesting it," Mrs. Pearson added, almost zombie-like, as she stared down at the bed.

"This is a cock-and-bull story if ever I have heard one. Where on earth would Mrs. Emerson have obtained a crossbow?" Daryll finally spoke up.

"Exactly Daryll, I'm sure if there was a crossbow on the premises, we would certainly have known about it." Mr. Pearson said.

"Ironically Daryll, it was provided by you!" Mario replied, "Claire, oh, I'm sorry, Miss Pearson, you said yourself that your great-grandmother ordered many of her craft supplies online now that she was housebound, so she was familiar with online ordering. I checked with security, they delivered a couriered package to Mrs. Emerson at 16:31 on the day in question. Daryll, you must remember bringing that package up to Mrs. Emerson." Daryll sat back in surprise as though he himself had been hit by a bolt as he remembered making that delivery. He had been sitting by Mrs. Emerson's bed with his right hand on the bed. Mrs. Emerson tapped his hand a couple of times to reassure him before returning her hand to her lap. A gesture that didn't go unnoticed by Mario. "Do you remember signing for the delivery of the package Mrs. Emerson? Prior to setting up the crossbow to begin practicing."

"So, it was a package, how can you be so sure it contained a crossbow?" Mr. Pearson intervened.

"There aren't that many archery stores in close proximity of the apartment building that would be able to satisfy a same-day delivery." Mario replied, 'Triggers & Bows', a small specialty store in Manhattan is one, I phoned them, they confirmed that a purchase of a crossbow was made and delivered to Mrs. Emerson, together with a crank. They explained how the crank worked and what little effort would be required to prime the bow, even by a frail, elderly, person. They informed me that they were instructed not to put a label on the box so that their name or the contents of the box would not be visible. There was just a handwritten name and address on an accompanying, sealed, envelope with the invoice inside. The reason for this, as explained to them by Mrs. Emerson, was that it was a surprise gift for someone. Once the crossbow had been ordered, Mrs. Emerson began to manufacture a number of ice-bolts to provide a suitable arsenal. On receipt of the weapon and after successfully assembling it, she executed a few practice shots, using her work board as a target."

"Wait a minute. What about Fletching?" The General asked, "you can't fire an arrow or a bolt without Fletching on them, they provide stability and accuracy. You told me yourself that there was no evidence of a weapon being found on the body, so, where are they? Answer me that." At this point, Darlene looked toward Pete as they stood by the door, hunched her shoulders and furrowed her brow, indicating to him that she had no idea what Fletching was. He mouthed 'feathers' and indicated with his fingers of one hand where they were on an arrow, using a straight finger on his other hand. Darlene didn't exactly reply, but shook her head from side to side and mouthed 'how do you know this shit'. Meanwhile, Mario continued with a reply to the General's question.

"No, General, they were not present, but with a powerful crossbow propelling a bolt at over 300 feet per second, the gentleman at 'Triggers & Bows' assured me that the absence of any Fletching at such a short-range would not be a significant factor," Mario explained, "that's another reason why Mrs. Emerson needed to practice so, she used her work board as a target. After all, who would question holes in a work board?"

"Despite the fact that all you have is the delivery of a package during the afternoon prior to the murder you have absolutely no evidence that Mrs. Emerson murdered Mr. Fearless. So, I will ask the obvious question, why on earth would Mrs. Emerson want to murder Mr. Fearless?" Haverly asked.

"Yes, that was another tough one until a snippet of information came to our attention. Funnily enough General, that also involved you. Coincidently, you had served with young Private Emerson in Vietnam," Mario said, "and at first, we considered that relationship as a line of investigation which we began to pursue. But after delving a little deeper we discovered that your relationship with Edgar was pure coincidence, a red herring. But what we did learn was that Edgar Emerson had been killed during the second phase of the Tet offensive on the 15th of May 1968."

"I fail to see what the significance of that is?" The General asked.

"It was the interview Mr. Fearless had with David Grover, the Vietnam vet. where he was badly embarrassed by Mr. Fearless. But that's not all, Mr. Fearless also slighted other Vietnam draftees which of course included Mrs. Emerson's son, he would have been one of those. The interview just happened to air on the night of the 15th, exactly fifty years since the death of Mrs. Emerson's only son." Mario replied, "I believe it was a little bit too much for Mrs. Emerson to bear."

There was a sudden silence in the room and for the first time, there was a tension in the air that was almost palpable and all that could be heard once more was the oxygen coursing through the tubes that led to Mrs. Emerson. For the first time, Mrs. Emerson looked away from Mario and down to her frail hands that were placed on her lap. A solitary tear appeared in her eye and slowly trickled down her sunken cheek. A movement that didn't go unnoticed by her granddaughter.

"Don't say, anything granny, all he has is circumstantial evidence, he can't prove a damn thing, he has no solid proof." Mrs. Pearson appealed to her grand-mother, sensing that the evidence was beginning to look favorable for a conviction.

"A few years ago, what you are suggesting would have been a true statement Mrs. Pearson, this would appear to have been a perfect crime, but in today's world, we have DNA analysis. We have enough data to prove Mrs. Emerson handled the bolt that penetrated the victim's chest," Mario said quietly and authoritatively, "we also have video evidence of the projectile traveling from Mrs. Emerson's apartment at a height consistent with someone in a wheelchair and disappearing through the doorway of the opposite apartment at precisely the level of the wound in Mr. Fearless's chest and at precisely the time of his death. Furthermore, the size of the projectile is not only consistent with an ice-bolt made from the cigar tube, but also of the fatal wound in Favio Fearless. Of course, due to the speed of the projectile, it would never have been noticed on the surveillance footage using normal techniques. We had to slow down the speed of the playback, even then, if we hadn't utilized the 60-inch HD screen in the apartment of Mr. Fearless we may still have missed it."

Once Mario had finished his dialogue nobody had any further arguments or obstacles to throw at his case, silence reigned, and they all kept alternating their looks to Mrs. Emerson and to one another. Finally, Mrs. Emerson broke the silence.

"So, what are you going to do detective, now that you know I am the guilty party? Arrest me and take me down to the station to lock me up?" Mrs. Emerson said hoarsely, taunting Mario. Then, with a great deal of effort and emotion, she tried to raise herself from the pillows as she continued, "my son was proud to fight for his country, he didn't try and shy away from his duty as that nasty man implied. I was not prepared to have the memory of my son tainted by such a waste of space as that man, so yes, I did it, I killed him. You have reconstructed the murder to a tee detective, but there is one thing you will never know." She paused to get her breath and everyone in the room was now looking directly at Mrs. Emerson, they were beside themselves with shock and surprise.

"After he unlocked his door, I called his name. He turned with that casual holier than thou mannerism he had until he saw that crossbow pointed directly at his chest. You should have seen the look on his face, at that moment, as brief as it was, it was one of total, helpless, fear." Mrs. Emerson's eyes had now closed to almost slits as she recalled the deed, her teeth were bared and her voice was almost hissing with venom, "it made up for all the terrible things that he had said to me and mine over the years. I had no compunction about pulling that trigger, to me it was all worthwhile, he was a nasty man."

The full realization of what Mrs. Emerson was saying, basically admitting to the crime and why she had done it, had now hit home to the others in the room. Mrs. Emerson sank back into the comfort of her pillows and closed her eyes, drained by the effort she had just displayed.

At first, Mario said nothing, he waited for everyone to digest the facts that they had just been dished up, then he addressed all the occupants in the room.

"Everyone, could you all leave the room, please, I would like to have a short, private interview with Mrs. Emerson," Mario said. Initially, Mario thought Mrs. Pearson was going to put up some type of protest, but under the circumstances, she decided against it, she appeared to be in a state of bewilderment. Pete opened the large door and Darlene stood on the opposite side and they waited as the others filed through the doorway into the corridor. Daryll was the last one of the group to exit and he was followed by Darlene with Pete closing the door behind him. Outside in the corridor, Pete and Darlene stood guard by the door to ensure the others did not make an unexpected attempt to return back in, although neither of the detectives knew exactly what was going on, they had been just as surprised as the others.

Inside the room, when they were both alone, Mario walked closer to the bed to ensure the group in the corridor could not hear what was about to be said.

"Mrs. Emerson, as untimely as Mr. Fearless's interview was with that vet. I think we both know, that wasn't the real reason for committing the murder, was it?" Mario asked gently.

"No, no it wasn't," Mrs. Emerson replied softly.

Chapter 27

"Mrs. Emerson, I have read the files Fearless had compiled about your family, he tried to blackmail you, didn't he?" Mario asked.

"Yes, he was a nasty man," she reiterated, "he wanted me to hand over the rights to the floor to him, in exchange, he would destroy the information he had attained concerning my family."

"And if you didn't co-operate?" Mario asked.

"Then he would use his TV program to broadcast all the dirt on the family, I couldn't let that happen," Mrs. Emerson explained, "although, I doubt now whether any of them will still want to live at the apartment after what has happened, so in a way, that bastard has got what he wanted, he has succeeded in getting us Emersons out of the building."

"But my understanding from the brief chat I'd had with Claire was that you just couldn't sign the rights over to him, there had to be some family involvement," Mario said.

"In that, you are absolutely correct detective," Mrs. Emerson replied, "he intended to get around that by marrying into the family with a very air-tight prenup, then after the marriage, as soon as the rights had been signed over to him, he would obtain a divorce, leaving my family with nothing."

"That's pretty ruthless," Mario said.

"Yes, it is, but it doesn't surprise me," Mrs. Emerson continued, "as I said, he was a nasty man."

"There's one more thing, the Vietnamese girl, Hang," Mario said.

"Oh, you mean Anne," Mrs. Emerson said with a smile, "yes, she's a lovely girl. Her mother brought her to see us just after General Haverly got them here from Vietnam, of course, he wasn't a General in those days. We couldn't call her Hang, so we used the name Anne and she used to visit us regularly, but it was only recently that she learned of her true relationship with us, just after her mother died." Mrs. Emerson paused for a little while to catch her breath and take a drink of water, which Mario assisted her with before she continued with her story, "they had settled into a small Vietnamese community in Chinatown here in New York and Anne's mother was a proud woman who refused all financial help from us. Instead, she managed to build up a successful office cleaning business that Anne inherited and still operates to this day. Anne's mother never married so everything was left to her daughter. Anne is happily married with two fine children, a boy, and a girl, my other great-grandchildren. They visit with me regularly, but can you believe they both enlisted in the army, so they are very rarely in town nowadays, but it's nice to have them with me right now. To finish up the story, Anne delegated others to run her company while she looks after me, the General and of course Mr. Fearless. He more or less blackmailed her into doing that. So, detective, I think that brings you right up to date."

"Yes, it does, but Mrs. Emerson, were any of the others aware of the information Fearless had on you?" Mario asked.

"About Anne yes, although they are not aware of the circumstances regarding Edgar's wedding to Avril, not even Angela knows that. No, I hadn't shared that information with any of the others, none of them know," Mrs. Emerson said, "but on the day before they were scheduled to bring me here, I instructed Claire to go over to Mr. Fearless's apartment to explain to him about my pending move. I also told her to tell him that he should ask her to bring him here to visit with me after I had settled in so that we could finalize matters."

"So, that was why Claire went to visit him in his apartment," Mario said rhetorically.

"Yes, but she never knew of the secret deal that Mr. Fearless had proposed, I was trying to lull him into a false sense of security, to let his guard down as it were. I thank you for not revealing the existence of the files to the rest of them. It was a clever ruse you came up with, my son being killed on that day, although I can't say I didn't think of him as I was pulling the trigger," Mrs. Emerson said as she thought about the memory of her son.

"So, when you sent Claire to visit Fearless, weren't you concerned that he would tell her of the proposition he had discussed with you, I mean marrying into the family?" Mario asked.

"No, not at all, it wasn't Claire he was hoping to marry, it was Michael," Mrs. Emerson replied.

Chapter 28

"It appears Mr. Fearless was a homosexual," Mrs. Emerson continued, using a different generation's vernacular, "and now that same-sex marriage was legal in New York he was hoping to marry Michael. He used to 'hit' on the poor boy at every available opportunity, even stalking him sometimes. That was why Michael moved to San Francisco. But once he had left, Fearless tracked him down and he kept calling him." That would account for the numerous calls to California that Fearless made, Mario thought as Mrs. Emerson continued, "then came the blackmailing, in an attempt to get me to arrange the wedding. Of course, I was never going to let that happen."

Were the surprises in this case ever going to end? Mario thought to himself. Now he felt bad, especially after thinking the worst when Claire had visited Fearless but now it seems she had been telling the truth.

"Do you think it was Avril who had given Fearless the information about the family?" Mario asked.

"Certain of it," Mrs. Emerson replied immediately and vehemently, "she was a vindictive, callous, bitch from the start, but when she received the letter from Edgar, telling her he was in love with an Asian girl she got worse. It got worse still when she found out that

Anne and her mother were spending time with us and we began to see less and less of her." She took another pause before continuing, "but I don't regret spending time with them, I can still vividly remember reading the letter from Edgar telling me about this girl he had met and how much in love he was with her. The words just skipped off the page with happiness, then when we first met her when she arrived in New York I understood why he was so much in love with her." She smiled at the memory and her eyes glazed over while she thought about that for a moment, "I still have the letter," and she reached into a pocket in the house-coat she was wearing and pulled out a well-worn envelope that appeared to contain an equally well-worn couple of pages and she held them up. "You see, I couldn't have these memories tainted by such a nasty man, now could I?" She secreted the envelope back in her pocket and then her demeanor changed as though she was having a pleasant conversation with a hospital visitor, she asked, "so, what's going to happen now, detective?"

"Just to make everything above board and proper, I will need a signed statement from you admitting to the murder of Mr. Fearless," Mario responded softly, "now, I just happen to have brought with me a form," Mario pulled out a lined sheet of paper from the inside pocket of his jacket, "if you could just sign at the bottom, you will have to trust me to type in the confession as you explained it to me earlier. Then I think we could leave you here to live out your last few days surrounded by your friends and family."

"After my confession, I don't think it really matters what you type on the form, do you?" Mrs. Emerson asked as she signed the paper.

"No, I guess not," Mario said, then he thanked her and walked over to the door, but before he opened it, he stopped to face Mrs. Emerson one last time.

"Detective, what will happen to the files Mr. Fearless created about my family?" Mrs. Emerson asked.

"They will remain our little secret Mrs. Emerson," Mario replied, "as nobody else is aware of the real motive for the murder and everyone thinks it was because of the interview on the 50th anniversary of the Tet offensive the dossiers no longer have any bearing on the case. Rest assured Mrs. Emerson, I will personally destroy the files."

"I thank you, detective," Mrs. Emerson replied. She believed Mario wholeheartedly and instantly relaxed in the knowledge that the secrets would never be divulged.

There was nothing further to be said between them, so Mario decided to take his leave.

"Goodbye Mrs. Emerson," Mario said then turned to open the door, "O.K. you can all come back in now," he told the others. Mrs. Pearson was the first one to return, she rushed through the door as if it was a

Le Mans start. Mario could hear her talking to her grand-mother as he left.

"Are you alright granny? What did he say to you?" Mrs. Pearson was asking as she arranged pillows and patted down the bed.

"Everything is fine dear, just sit down and stop fussing," Mrs. Emerson could be heard saying.

The three detectives retraced their steps down the corridor and out of the building towards the car park. Outside the hospice, Darlene appeared to be a little confused.

"Boss, there are still a couple of things I don't quite understand. Where and when did Harry get DNA samples from Mrs. Emerson to compare them to the foreign DNA found in Fearless's body?" Darlene asked.

"She didn't," Mario said simply, leaving a bemused Darlene behind him as he continued to walk towards his car.

Chapter 29

Darlene quickly caught up with Mario, "I don't get it boss, so, how can forensics possibly know that the DNA found in Fearless's body was that of Mrs. Emerson?" She asked, pursuing her line of thought.

"They don't," Mario said with a slight smile on his face, as they reached the car, he was enjoying teasing the rookie.

"But didn't you just say in there that you had enough DNA evidence to prove she handled the bolt," Darlene said.

"He did," Pete said with a knowing smile.

"I did," Mario replied, he was now standing on the driver's side of his vehicle looking directly across the roof of the car at Darlene, who was preparing to get into the rear of the car on the other side. "It was all pure bluff, I called Harry as soon as I suspected how the murder had been carried out, but she told me it would be like searching for a needle in a haystack. Under the scenario I described to her, she told me that the chances of finding any foreign DNA in the wound from a once frozen tube of water would be almost infinitesimal if not impossible. Now, if it was a real bolt that had been fired, it would have been different, but of course, had it have been a real bolt we would have worked it out a hell of a lot sooner."

"So, if Mrs. Emerson hadn't have owned up to it, we would have nothing," Darlene almost whispered.

"You got it," Mario replied and they both got into the car with Pete in the passenger seat, but then Mario turned to Darlene. "Don't fret yourself, we would have gotten her eventually," Mario stressed, "once we had cracked the *'how'* and the *'who'* we would have found enough evidence to pin it on her, but fortunately, now, we don't have to."

"So, what was it that triggered your suspicions boss?" Pete asked.

"When you said you were going to bring me into the 21st Century," Mario replied, "that was exactly the expression Claire used when she bought Mrs. Emerson an iPad. It was then that all the tumblers fell into place."

On the trip back to the precinct, Mario called his Chief to tell him the good news, Horowitz congratulated them all and was immediately going to call the Commissioner. After the call to his chief, Mario explained to Pete and Darlene the real reason why Mrs. Emerson murdered Mr. Fearless and repeated his private conversation with Mrs. Emerson. The two detectives were both as surprised as Mario was when they heard about the scheming plan Mr. Fearless had tried to concoct to obtain ownership of the penthouse suites. Finally, Mario told the other two of his intention to shred the dossiers Fearless had compiled on the Emersons. He was going to stick with the original motive for Mrs. Emerson murdering Fearless, which was his interview on the anniversary of her son's death. Although the dossiers provided the final piece of the puzzle in solving the crime; as far as Mario was concerned, there was no reason to mention them in their final reports. There was no disagreement from Pete or Darlene and very little more was said until they entered the underground car park at the precinct and parked the car.

They made their way up to the office where instead of being met by jubilant cheers and slaps on the back they were met by an empty office. Even Horowitz had been told to go over to the Commissioner's office to attend the press conference to announce the solving of the case. To add insult to injury, their inboxes were inundated with useless, irrelevant office memos and they had numerous calls on their voicemails to attend to. Such are the trials and tribulations of a homicide detective. In some ways, the empty office was a blessing as it gave Mario the opportunity to walk over to the stationary room and shred the Emerson dossiers without any curious eyes around to wonder what he was doing. Once Mario had finished destroying the papers he returned to his desk and more or less fell into his desk-chair and looked at his blinking phone with its plethora of calls. Then he saw the memos, how many memos can the precinct produce in 24 hours? He thought. Then he looked at the clock on the wall and remembered that the last time he gazed at that clock he had been looking forward to going for a beer. Apart from the time, nothing had changed.

"O.K. let's get outta here," Mario shouted to the others and they followed him like doting hounds to the watering hole known as Clancy's.

Conclusion

Mrs. Emerson's organs began to fail the day after she signed her statement and she passed away less than 48 hours after being charged with the murder of Favio Fearless. Mario managed to hold off the baying dogs of the media until after her death was confirmed so she never saw the newspaper headlines nor her character assassination on the TV stations.

Avril had died of liver failure a few weeks before Fearless's murder, so her secrets went with her to her grave. More significantly, that left Fearless alone in knowing about the skeletons in the Emerson's cupboard so, with his murder and the destruction of the dossiers, the information would never surface again.

With the death of Mrs. Emerson, Angela Pearson became the beneficiary of a large sum of tax-free money courtesy of a very good insurance policy written up by Ralph Emerson. That wasn't all, Mrs. Emerson had been correct about the apartment, in the months that followed, the Pearson family decided that, under the circumstances, continuing to own the residence was not in their best interests. They now thought it was extremely doubtful that any of the family would ever return to live in New York again, so they felt it would be best to negotiate the sale of the apartment with the owners of the building. Consequently, the Pearsons received another large sum of cash and in turn, the property management team ripped out the two penthouse apartments and replaced them with ten new luxurious ones, although they did manage to salvage the gym that Fearless had created and continued to use it as an elite spa. The property management company succeeded in maintaining a private luxurious image, and as a result, was able to charge exorbitant rents. They also replaced the plate in the elevator to read 'Penthouse Suites' and Daryll secured a cushy little position as the Concierge for the elite residents on that floor. In turn, Brad was promoted to Security Supervisor and Fred became Shift Supervisor. Daryll never saw Mrs. Pearson again and whether any of the Pearson family were aware of the dossiers that had been compiled about them or Mr. Emerson, was left to conjecture.

General Haverly's life went on unchanged, he remained in his apartment and continued to receive offers to contribute to various TV programs, magazines and newspaper columns. Although the General did decide to negotiate a new cleaning service, he didn't think it was worth Anne turning up at the building to do just his apartment. But that didn't mean he lost contact with Anne and her children, he continued to act as the perfect Godfather to her and her children, in memory of his late friend Edgar, and he followed their military careers closely. Whenever they were in town, he would meet with them for lunch or dinner, together with Anne and her husband.

Claire did indeed upgrade to another apartment but decided to remain in Boston. The money her parents received from the insurance policy and the sale of the apartment provided the rent for the upgraded accommodation plus a generous amount left over for living expenses, an equal sum was paid to her brother, Michael. Mario never saw Claire again, he would like to have done and often thought about contacting her, but he felt charging her great-grandmother with murder had created an awkward situation that negated any further development of a possible relationship.

As for Grover and his cronies, the opprobrium did indeed manifest itself, they continued to be investigated, but rather than press charges and to avoid publicity, the credit card companies arranged a repayment schedule with the culprits. Part of the deal was that Grover would refund all the donations received, retire from public speaking and never make any future public engagements.

David Johnstone, Fearless's loyal producer, was offered a position on one of the nationally broadcasted late shows that were based on the west coast. David and his family moved out to California and he made a successful life in the sunshine.

The Favio Fearless estate turned out to be a more difficult matter that was to take took a couple of years to resolve. With no living parents, no heirs and no will in place, there began a legal battle as to who was the lawful recipient of the millions that were held in bank accounts and investment accounts in both the U.S. and the U.K. Eventually, the proceeds, less substantial legal fees and government taxes from both the U.S. and the U.K., ended up being divided between the two siblings of Fearless's mother. Despite the costs incurred, the net proceeds received by each of the two siblings were still a sizeable amount.

Despite all the praise that had been lauded upon the team of detectives from both within the precinct and the media for the speedy resolution of the case, Darlene was not a happy camper. She didn't feel she had contributed anything towards the solving of the crime, she was also under the impression that the guys really didn't want another member intruding on their team, especially that of a young woman, still a bit wet behind the ears. Her senses told her that they enjoyed being a duo and were quite happy to remain that way. As a result, a few days after the media announcement had been made, while they were all in the office wrapping up the paperwork, Darlene approached the two detectives as they were leaning over Mario's desk, reviewing some of the final reports that were laid out there.

"Excuse me guys, but I have something to tell you," Darlene said, and the two detectives slowly turned their heads to face her, "after giving it a lot of thought I've decided that I'm going to put in a transfer request."

"What? Why do you want to leave us?" I thought you wanted to be assigned to homicide." Mario's voice had raised an octave or two in response to the surprising request, both men stood to their full height in astonishment, demanding to know the reason for her decision to leave them.

"Look, let's face it, you guys don't really want me around, I feel I'm just making up the numbers here," Darlene replied.

"Have we said that?" Pete asked with a directness that surprised her.

"No, you don't have to, it's just there," Darlene stated.

"What's there?" Mario asked instantly, putting Darlene unexpectedly on the spot.

"It doesn't matter, I don't feel I contributed anything to the solving of the case," Darlene said, "you really don't need me on your team." She looked down at the notebook in her hands as she continued to flip the pages as though an important clue was about to jump out and justify her presence on the team. Not being able to think of anything further to say she started to turn away from the two men, but Pete came around from the other side of the desk with a speed and a deftness that surprised her and in doing so, he blocked her path.

"You mean, like me!" Pete said, pointing to himself, "what did I contribute eh? It was genius here who cracked the case," motioning his head towards Mario.

"But could I have done that without all the intel. I was receiving from the pair of you?" Mario asked, "no! In fact, you were the first one to suggest that Fearless could have been killed by a projectile fired from the other apartment? Do you think that suggestion went unnoticed?"

"But you more or less disregarded it at the time!" Darlene stated, holding out her arms as she recalled the conversation.

"You're right, Darlene I did, but I did give it some thought, at that time, based on the evidence we had gathered, it wasn't considered possible. But discounted? Absolutely not." Mario stressed.

"That's how crime teams operate Darlene," Pete added, "we brainstorm, we run through relevant and irrelevant information, we throw out stupid and sound scenarios until we get down to the real nitty-gritty. As we discover new evidence, we re-cycle some of the previously discarded scenarios to see if they will fit with the new information. That's exactly what we did in this case, and you contributed to that, big time." Pete stressed, now pointing his finger at Darlene.

"As for not wanting you on the team, that's simply not true. Neither of us has ever said anything negative about you joining us, right Pete?" Mario said, looking at Pete. Pete, in turn, stood shaking his head. "Now, if you still want to quit," emphasizing the word in a way that would suggest Darlene was giving up, "well, I won't stand in your way," Mario continued, "but you're an excellent detective Darlene, don't sell yourself short, you did good on this case, a great asset to the team. I think it would be a huge mistake for you to leave." There was a slight pause as Darlene stood mulling over what Mario and Pete had said. She was both pleasantly surprised and ecstatic at the positive reaction she was receiving from the two men, she certainly hadn't expected that.

"That's so sweet of you both, to say such kind words," Darlene said, her voice cracking slightly as she fought back the tears of joy. Then Pete decided to provide some additional insight for her to consider.

"And anyway, we still need someone to get the coffees and donuts!" Pete said.

"Yeah, there is that too!" Mario added flippantly. Darlene began to seethe, she stood with her hands on her hips and was about to give them both a piece of her mind, but before she could, she was distracted by Humph entering their office laboring with a huge bunch of flowers.

"Darlene, my dear girl, there you are," Humph said, "I thought that after the successful completion of your first case with these reprobates I would bring you this floral gift to officially welcome you to the team. As I told you before when we first met, you're like a rose between two thorns, so, I thought only roses would be appropriate!" Darlene gasped at the sight of the various, colored flowers and any thoughts about leaving the department had now quickly vanished.

"Thank you Humph, they're lovely!" Darlene responded as she accepted the bouquet from Humph who was wearing a white tie embroidered with red roses to suit the occasion.

"You'd better watch out with Humph, Darlene," Pete said, "you know how the rose is alleged to have been created? The God Zephyrus loved Flora, the Goddess of Flowers, so much so that he changed himself into a rose because the Goddess had no interest in anything other than flowers. When Flora saw the rose, she kissed it and thus fulfilled Zephyrus' wish. I think Humph thinks he's Zephyrus." Darlene didn't care, she was too delighted and responded by fulfilling the prophecy and giving Humph a kiss on his cheek. That made Humph's day and he smiled like the proverbial cat that got the cream before turning to Pete with a quizzical look on his face.

"How do you know all this shit?" Humph asked. Pete just shrugged his shoulders in response.

"I'll have to put these into a vase, they're lovely," Darlene said, still slightly overcome by the gift.

"You might find a vase in one of the kitchen cupboards," Mario told her. Darlene walked over to the kitchen with the flowers and she did indeed find a vase in the cupboard under the sink. It had obviously not been used in some considerable time, so she had to give it a thorough clean before beginning to place the roses into it.

Once Darlene was out of earshot Pete took the opportunity to tell one of his stories.

"That reminds me," Pete began while Mario and Humph rolled their eyes, knowing full well that a joke was coming, "a brunette and a blonde were discussing their upcoming weekend plans and the brunette said, 'my boyfriend just bought me a big bunch of flowers so I guess I'll be spending my weekend on my back with my legs up in the air.' The blonde replied, 'why, don't you have a vase?'" They all laughed until Humph brought up the topic of the chief's absence.

"By the way, where's ornery, old, Horowitz?" Humph asked Mario as he looked around the floor, "I didn't see him in his office when I came by!"

"Haven't seen him all morning," Mario replied, "we received word there was a big meeting being held early this morning over at the commissioner's office. All department heads were told to be there."

"Something big then?" Humph inquired.

"Could be, I know as much as you do," Mario replied.

"Well, I think this is bad pool," Humph replied, feigning exasperation, "the least the chief could do is spot us all for lunch for a job well done!" Just then, the slamming of a door was heard, and Chief Horowitz came blundering into the office. Darlene finished her flower arranging and carried the vase over to her desk to await the Chief's arrival into their area.

As the Chief walked towards them, they could all immediately tell from his mannerisms and the stern look on his craggy face that it was going to be business as usual. They would be lucky to even get a pizza delivery that day, let alone go out for a celebratory lunch.

The End

ACKNOWLEDGEMENTS

The author wishes to thank the following for their technical expertise:

Fred Galati (retired policeman, Punta Gorda, Florida) for his insights into police investigations.

Anthony Dickson (Triggers & Bows, Burford, Ontario) for his assistance regarding crossbow expertise.

Lori Blanchard (Hamilton Archery Centre, Hamilton Ontario) for helping me get the *point*.

Terry Connolly (Family) for reading the draft and making suggestions.

Needless to say, any errors or omissions in the novel regarding the above areas of expertise remain the fault of the author.

AVAILABLE SOON:

Genesis Déjà vu – The Early Years (the third book in the series)

Murder of a Multitude (another Mario Simpson mystery)

To join the mailing list, email:

DEXTER-JAMES@OUTLOOK.COM

Manufactured by Amazon.ca
Bolton, ON